FORT FISHER

The Battle for the Gibraltar of the South

FORT FISHER

THE BATTLE FOR THE GIBRALTAR OF THE SOUTH

BY

GREG AHLGREN

P

Pen-L Publishing
Fayetteville, AR
Pen-L.com

ISBN: 978-1-942428-73-2
First edition
Printed and bound in the USA

Front cover artwork: U.S. Naval History and Heritage Command Photograph: NH 2051 *The Bombardment of Fort Fisher*, January 15, 1865 Engraving by T. Shussler, after an artwork by J.O. Davidson

Back cover artwork: Chicago : Kurz & Allison, Art Publishers, 1890.
http://hdl.loc.gov/loc.pnp/pga.01862

Cover and interior design by Kelsey Rice

ACKNOWLEDGMENTS

So many good people have been generous in providing comments, suggestions, encouragement, and assistance for this book that it is impossible to list them all. However, a special debt of gratitude is owed for the literary critique of Stephen Monier, the technical expertise on Civil War firearms and armaments provided by Dr. Richard Deveaux, the literary input and stylistic advice of America's leading techno-thriller author, Helen Hanson, and finally, once again, to my good friend Bennett Freeman, whose creative and literary input has been invaluable. All of you helped make this book possible. To all, I say thank you.

PROLOGUE

Wilmington, North Carolina
Thursday, January 12, 1865
Dawn

His mother gave him a last, lingering hug, her eyes welling up as she released him.

"Must you go back?" She reached with her right hand for the arm of the chair behind her. Using her left to steady her cane, she settled on the wicker rocker thick with pillows that had stood in front of the fireplace for as long as Caleb Cuthbait could remember.

"Mother," he said, "I will not desert. And I need to go now or I may miss the early steamer."

"I'll walk down with him," Caleb's father interjected. "You rest awhile, dear, and I'll make us some tea when I return." He tenderly covered his wife's shoulders with her shawl. "Warm enough?" He kissed her lightly on the cheek.

She adjusted the shawl, covering the threadbare elbows of her cotton dress. The dress had not been replaced in several years, but Caleb knew that getting textile goods to make a new one was nearly impossible.

"Yes, thank you," his mother said. "Oh! I nearly forgot. I set some salted pork on the table, Caleb. Take it. I imagine it is a far sight better than your rations at the fort."

Caleb retrieved the paper-wrapped meat from the pantry and took a last look around his parents' home. His father was already standing by the door. Caleb buttoned his gray tunic against the chill of the winter morning and stepped outside.

From the Cuthbait home at Wilmington's northern edge, the pair walked a zigzag pattern toward the landing, heading south on the numbered streets that paralleled the Cape Fear River and west on the named ones. Caleb remembered it as the same route he had walked with his father four years earlier on a humid, late-summer afternoon as he headed off to college. On that day, everyone they passed had been an acquaintance of his father's, and all knew where Caleb was going. They stepped from their neatly trimmed homes and cottages to stop the father and son, tipping their hats to their minister while clapping Caleb on the back and wishing him well. War was in the air, but in Wilmington, North Carolina, on that August afternoon, the hope of a compromise reigned supreme.

Now, many of these same houses were shuttered. Yards were overgrown, and paint peeled from the clapboards. Those who could afford to had left, seeking shelter with friends or relatives where the threat of battle was lower.

Some had rented out their homes, and a tenancy of profiteers, blockade runners, and those who earned a living off them, had taken their place. Although liquor and wild parties flowed freely, yard work and housekeeping held little value for the city's present occupants.

As Caleb walked toward the landing, his father's normally booming voice was soft in his ear.

"You have a good heart, Son. The widow, Missus Tuckerman, will be lucky to have you. It means a great deal to your mother and me that you're using your grandmother's band. I expect your mother's tears told you that pretty well. I wish, though, that you could properly ask her father's blessing."

"That's a little difficult right now, Father."

Reverend Cuthbait nodded. "Everyone knew Captain Tuckerman's reputation. She must be a strong woman to have stayed."

"Now, Father," Caleb protested. "I'm only taking the ring in case. I've not fully made up my mind on this. And I would hope to ask her father, but circumstances make it impossible. I'm certain a Confederate soldier from North Carolina would be stopped well before reaching Connecticut," he added with a smirk.

They continued in silence. At Dock Street, the pair turned right, heading straight for the river. Rounding the corner, Caleb spotted a still figure lying in the dirt at the side of the road, arms positioned wildly over his head. At first, Caleb feared he was dead, but as he stepped quickly toward him, he discerned the loud snoring of a drunk. Striding past, he smelled the stale vomit that stained the seaman's clothing. He assumed him to be from the British blockade runner tied at the docks.

One block from the landing, three more sailors surrounded a woman lounging back against the wall of a saloon—her face heavily made up, and her lips painted red.

"A little early in the morning for this, wouldn't you say?" his father asked.

Caleb smiled. "I think, for some, it's still last night."

The wharf was soon in sight. The steamer's boiler belched black smoke, and the crew knelt along the dock, unwrapping lines from the cleats.

Caleb stopped at the edge of the wharf, and a step later, his father did the same, turning to his son with a quizzical expression.

"What is it?"

"How do I know? How do I know if she is the right woman?"

His father smiled broadly. "If you ask twelve people, you'll get a dozen answers. But as you're asking me, I tell you to look in your heart. If you love her, if your life will be richer with her by your side, if you would give your soul to save hers, and if you believe she feels the same of you, then you're on the right track. This is a big step, Caleb, and I am glad you're not taking it lightly. I only wish you had thought as long before joining the army."

"Father, we have been over this," Caleb sighed.

His father held his hands up, palms outward. "Yes, yes, I know. But you're our only child. At Christmas, we could hear the bombardment. We had no peace for days until we knew you were unharmed. Perhaps you can get another day of leave soon. Bring Missus Tuckerman to church. We would love to meet her. And now you'd best be off," his father said as the sailors tossed the lines over the rails and scrambled after them. "The steamer keeps to its schedule, not yours."

Caleb nodded, hugged his father, and ran across the wharf, jumping onto the deck of the paddle steamer just as her whistle blew.

In a few hours, he knew, he would be back at Fort Fisher.

CHAPTER 1

The first boiler was already starting to sear.

Fireman Patrick Sheedy felt the heat burning his face. With a gloved hand, he reached out and closed the damper several inches, restricting the air supply to the inferno. He turned back to the two coal heavers on his shift and shook his head.

Seeing his fireman close the damper, Nat Davis drove his shovel into the coal in the bunker beneath his feet. He yanked a soiled rag from his pocket and wiped the sweat that beaded across his forehead. At the rear of the bunker, Sven Johanson stood with his back to the boiler, using his shovel to drag coal to the front.

"Sven!" Patrick yelled.

When the tall heaver turned questioningly, the fireman waved a stop. Sven pitched his shovel into the black mass at his feet and stepped forward.

"What you figure, boss?" Nat asked.

"I think we be making seven knots," Patrick answered. "Maybe eight."

Nat coughed and continued to wipe his face. Despite the raw January morning weather off the North Carolina coast, the temperature in the boiler room was already well over one hundred degrees. Given the right climate and need for speed, it could easily reach one hundred twenty.

"I don't think Captain Guest wants us to set his boat afire," Nat said.

He coughed again and turned to spit back into the bunker. Stripped to his waist, the motion exposed Nat's back to his fireman, and Patrick stared once again at the scars that crisscrossed the coal heaver's back. There was a darker purple one that extended down from his left shoulder that, during especially vigorous shoveling, could still pull apart and bleed. The fireman knew Nat's story—as he knew that of nearly every man on the *Iosco*—and he was constantly amazed at the punishment and torture so many slaves had endured prior to escaping north.

"Ja, I've seen it," Sven said. He looked around the cramped boiler room and gestured. "A wooden boat, it catch the fire."

"And an iron one can scald a man fifty feet from the boiler," Patrick said. "When she starts firing up on a good run, the boilers can run red, and then the iron starts glowing past the boiler room, into the mess, everywhere."

"We almost done, boss," Nat said.

Patrick Sheedy nodded. "The boatswain'll be piping shift any minute now."

As if on cue, Andy Wilson appeared in the hatchway, followed by his own two coal heavers, both contrabands. There were fourteen Negroes—escaped slaves and free men—out of the ship's total crew of one hundred seventy-three. Ten of them served as heavers.

"You leave me any steam," Wilson asked, "or you girls just lollygagging through your shift?"

"Aye, y' got plenty," Patrick answered. "She's starting to run hot, so I closed her down a bit."

Wilson pushed past the fireman he was replacing and squinted into the fire pit that glowed bright red. The two replacement coal heavers hung back at the hatch.

After a moment, Wilson turned around.

"What do you hear, Sheedy?" he asked in a low voice.

"I hear me lunch a-calling. That's what I hear."

"To hell with you. I'm serious."

"I'm serious too."

Wilson pointed to the deck over his head. "Your Mick friend Flanagan seems to have his ear everywhere, what does he say? We going back?"

Behind him, Patrick sensed his own two coal heavers stiffen. At four o'clock that morning, the boatswain had piped the crew out of their hammocks. The *Iosco* rocked at anchor in the Beaufort, North Carolina, harbor, which had been in Union hands since March of '62 and now served as a Union naval base for the North Atlantic Blockading Squadron. The night had been rough. A severe storm had tumbled men from their hammocks and left them cursing in four languages.

But the crew had assembled to a calmer sea and, as they did every day, commenced to holystone the deck and scrub and polish the brass in the predawn light. But as Patrick Sheedy joined the rest of the crew in their grumbling acquiescence to busywork, he sensed a difference. Troopships had arrived in Beaufort from Hampton Roads a few days earlier. It was rumored they would head to Charleston or support Sherman's march through Georgia. Would the navy be going with them?

On the foredeck, Captain John Guest huddled with his highest officers, an open chart held in both hands. The officers nodded as he spoke.

The harbor had seemed different too. There were always ships, but today, the number of visible warship signal lamps, in addition to the troopships, appeared much greater.

At breakfast, Ensign Feilberg had approached Patrick and leaned in close. "You have the first shift today," he said.

"Aye," he responded through a mouthful of moldy bread.

"Make haste," the ensign hissed in his ear. "The captain wants full steam brought up quick. We're weighing anchor and sliding out with the light." Feilberg spun about smartly and strode out of the crew's mess.

Although on some ships crews were segregated, particularly on the river gunboats that prowled southern inland waters, the *Iosco* was fully integrated. Those who shifted together, ate together, regardless of race. After the ensign's departure, Patrick grabbed his two coal heavers—one white, one black—and the three had made their way aft to the boiler room to begin their four-hour shift.

The question was on everyone's mind, but no one had spoken of it until Fireman Wilson's appearance.

"Whether we be going back or not is not up to us lowly tars, you know that, Mister Wilson."

"To hell with you," Wilson grumbled again.

When he heard the boatswain pipe the shift change, Patrick nodded at his two coal heavers and gestured. They lifted their shovels out of the coal mass and, stepping out of the bunker, handed them to their replacements.

"It's not hell I'm going to, laddie, it's dinner." Patrick tugged on his shirt and jacket and led his two coal heavers out of the boiler room and back to their mess. Seamus Flanagan was already seated, a plate full of beans and rice in front of him.

"It's true," he muttered as Patrick entered.

"What is?"

"What Wilson was asking you about," Seamus answered.

Patrick grunted and moved to the edge of the room, where he grabbed his plate and utensils from his own mess kit. Draping a leg over the bench, he sat facing the older sailor. Seamus held the higher rank of ordinary seaman, due to his three years on sailing ships prior to enlistment.

"How do you know?" Patrick asked.

Seamus let out a large burp. "Last night," he began, "the captain had two boys row him ashore, Tommy Waddel and little Mikey."

"Just the captain?"

"Aye."

Patrick scoffed. "What, did the captain let little Mikey into the brass's meeting room?"

"No, but Admiral Porter had two sailors row himself ashore from the *Malvern*. They talked to Tommy while the captains met. We're going back to Fort Fisher. Again. With more ships. And more men. We're to take the fort this time."

Patrick raised an eyebrow. "And, pray tell, what will be different now?"

"Well, first of all, me boy, Major General Benjamin Butler will no longer be in command. General Grant done replaced him with Major General Alfred Terry and give the good general nine thousand troops from the Army of the James."

"And are they walking there?" Patrick asked, reaching for a piece of bread in the middle of the table.

"They're already aboard."

Patrick stopped his hand halfway to the bowl.

"Aboard?"

Seamus nodded. "That's right. The ones who were loaded onto transports at Hampton Roads six days ago and been with us in Beaufort. Nine thousand men. And there will be almost sixty ships this time, and we're to give the rebs one hell of a going-over from the gunboats, all a-firing at once on the fort. Drive Johnny Reb and his kind off the guns so's they can't shoot back and then level the fort, taking out as many of their big guns as we can. And the lads will walk right up and close it down."

"Nine thousand, you say?"

"Aye, and that's not the half of it. That's just from the army. Tommy said the admiral was going to add another thousand sailors and marines from the boats and put them ashore also, to back up the soldiers. Men who won't be needed when our guns are a-firing. So, there'll be about ten thousand all fighting at once. We'll take that fort this time, and when we do, Patrick, that'll be the end of the grays. Wilmington is their last open port. You know as well as I do that our blockade has closed all the others, and this fort guards the mouth of the Cape Fear River. We take this fort, and the river is closed. Johnny can't get no supplies up to Wilmington, and Robert E. Lee runs dry in just a few months, maybe a few weeks. And then we all go home."

"They say the fort can't be taken," Patrick said. "Look what happened last month. They say it's the 'Gibraltar of the New World.'"

Seamus shook his head. "It'll be taken."

"That's what they told us last month," Patrick said. "Two days we bombed it, right through Christmas Day, and what'd we get? Our mast shot off, and then Johnny Reb struts some victory cannon shots as we slunk away."

"I'd go."

The pair turned to look at Nat Davis, who had stopped eating and was staring at them intently.

"Go?" Seamus asked.

Nat pointed toward the front of the ship. "On the shore. Grab a rifle and shoot. I'd trade my shovel for a gun."

Landsman Vranken roared from the other end of the mess table. "You niggers just want to kill Southerners! All of you. Well, go ahead, but some of us white folk just want to stay alive."

The Negro coal heaver started to rise, but Seamus laid a kindly hand on his shoulder.

"Careful who you be calling a nigger, Mister Vranken. It seems to me we all be working for a massa down here, except some of us have more personal cause to do so, if you know what I be meaning."

"Aye," another landsman, Jeremiah Phillips, joined in. "We white folks didn't enlist in this navy to do fighting, leastways not to get shot at."

"So, why'd you enlist then, Phillips, me boy?" Seamus asked, twisting sideways to the other landsman. "Someone ply you with liquor at the Boston *Rendezvous*, tell you they'd find you a woman, and then you woke up on the deck of the *Ohio*?"

The sailors around the table roared with laughter.

"For the prize money," Vranken responded, turning red. "That's what they told us, lots of prize money for every blockade runner we catch, a portion of the cargo divvied up in cash, and iron sides to protect us in a fight." The landsman scoffed. "And this ship ain't even iron. Even though she's a new one."

"Ha! And when do we get our money?" Phillips demanded.

The comment was met with grumbled assent.

"It's been what, two months since we took the *Sybil*?" Phillips asked. "She had three hundred and seven bales of cotton, that's worth a bit. And we ain't seen none of it."

"And we ain't been paid yet, not for two months," Vranken added. "I ain't seen my twelve dollars since November."

There was more grumbling, interrupted when Ensign Jameson poked his head in the door and turned his attention to Patrick and Seamus.

"Sheedy, Flanagan, the captain wants to see you, and be quick about it."

CHAPTER 2

Federal Point, North Carolina

January 12, 1865

Late morning

"You really need that fire today?"

Elizabeth Tuckerman prodded a log through the grate with her metal tongs. It rolled, and sparks raced up the flue. She answered without looking back at her visitor.

"I can't always count on getting a new one going easily, being all alone and all. Better to not let this one go out."

Caleb Cuthbait swallowed but said nothing. He stood awkwardly in the doorway, as if awaiting an order from his lieutenant.

Apparently satisfied with the invigorated fire, Elizabeth stood and wiped her hands across her apron. She turned to face Caleb.

"So, how was your three-day pass to Wilmington?" she asked.

Caleb shrugged. "It was fine." He reached into his pocket and felt for the ring.

"And you didn't consider perhaps spending some of that time here?" she asked.

Caleb drew in a quick breath. He didn't want a fight. Not now. Not on his way back to the fort. There had been enough of them recently with Elizabeth, and God knew there might yet be another big one coming at the fort itself soon. He had gotten off the river steamer at the landing just below her cottage and assumed that she'd be glad to see him—appreciative that he had stopped in on his way back, even though it meant that he'd now have to travel the last five miles down the peninsula on foot to get back by noon. He left the ring in his pocket and withdrew his hand.

Why couldn't she understand? She had been married herself once, to a river captain. He had died of yellow fever in the 1862 epidemic. She was four years older than Caleb, but he didn't care—not about that, not that she was a widow, not even that she was a Yankee. He just didn't understand why she always seemed so eager to pick a fight.

"I thought it important to see my parents," he said.

She nodded at the straight-back chair in the corner, away from the fire. He took it as an invitation and settled himself on it.

"And how are the Reverend and Missus Cuthbait?" she asked.

"Well, my mother has been sick this whole winter. She got the pleurisy, and raw weather makes it hard for her to get around. It's been difficult on my father. That's why I spent the three days with them. Cut some firewood, repaired their roof. Father has a lot to manage."

He thought his response clever and hoped she would see the selfishness of her pique. If she did, her expression didn't betray it.

"Tsk, tsk," she said sympathetically. "And Reverend Cuthbait not having a house slave to help with his wife."

Caleb grew hot. "Now Missus Tuckerman, you know well enough that my father does not cater to slavery. He will not."

She placed her hands on her hips. "So now it's *Missus* Tuckerman? And what about his son?" she asked.

Caleb drew a deeper breath. Perhaps he should've taken the supply steamer all the way to the fort and avoided all this.

"You know I don't own any slaves," he said.

Elizabeth nodded. "Of course I know that. But what I don't know is whether you don't own any *yet*."

No, maybe this is what attracted him to her after all, he thought. Elizabeth Tuckerman wasn't like the other eligible women he knew in Wilmington. She was feisty, always ready to argue. He didn't exactly like the arguments, but she was always interesting and ready to challenge him.

"I don't take to slavery either," he responded. "You know that well enough."

She raised her eyebrows. "So then tell me again, Mister Caleb Cuthbait, what you're doing in that rebel uniform."

He sighed and moved his hands out to his sides expansively before bringing them back and folding them across his chest.

"We've had this discussion many times, Missus Tuckerman. Let me ask you something," he said, leaning forward. "You come down here from Hazardville, Connecticut, the heart of abolitionist territory, and marry a Southern man, a riverboat captain even, who makes his living by transporting goods, including slaves, up and down the Cape Fear River. Did you argue with him about this, or is it just with me?"

Immediately, he realized his mistake. She turned away quickly as her eyes misted over. She went to the rocker in the opposite corner and sat to regain her composure.

"Frederick Tuckerman was a hard man," she said.

"I know, Elizabeth, I'm sorry. I didn't mean—" he began, but she cut him off with a wave of her hand.

"I've told you all this," she said. "A very hard man, especially when he had liquor."

"I know, I . . . I'm sorry," he stammered.

"I did my duty as his wife. When he took ill, I nursed him and did everything that was needed. He was out of work, and I took what I had from my seamstress work and made sure the doctor was here. But I'll tell you true, Caleb, I felt relief when the doctor pronounced him dead."

Caleb did not respond. He heard the heavy ticking of the clock on the mantel, and he turned to it. It was a Waterbury, and he assumed Elizabeth brought it south with her when she had arrived as a twenty-year-old bride.

He couldn't leave like this, so he changed the subject.

"How is your seamstress work?" he asked. "That is, when you're not riding that horse of yours up and down the peninsula. I know several of the officers at the fort have had you make them new uniforms."

Elizabeth brightened, and if she were still thinking of her late husband, her face did not reveal it.

"Talking about me, are you? Down there?" she challenged in a suddenly playful tone.

"Well, several of the officers think themselves proud that a Yankee seamstress made them their new uniforms."

"Proud is not the word. I would say more gloating. And they didn't have a lot of choice. I'm the only one around who has the red flannel lining for the artillery officers' uniforms."

Despite the awkwardness, he chuckled. "And that's not all true. They come down from Wilmington too. Why, I heard that a local band of citizens up there came to you to make General Braxton Bragg's new uniform, the one he's been showing off at all those parades of his."

"Oh, I've heard about the parades, and the officers' balls they've been having in Wilmington," she pouted. "Doesn't seem like there's been much use put to your rebel army up there, marching about and dancing."

"Well, rumor has it that Bragg will be sending Hoke's division north in a few days to attack the Yankees at New Bern. That will end the parades. At least, that's what my officers think."

"And, pray tell," she teased, "what do those same officers think of their sergeant being a Northern-educated man?"

Caleb shrugged. "I would hardly say that half a year at a college in Maine makes me educated, Northern or otherwise."

"Yes," she laughed, as if she had by now put the whole unpleasant topic of her husband behind her. "But what a college. Bowdoin, of all places. Why, isn't that the very college where that Professor Chamberlain taught, whose praises all the Northern papers have been singing for almost two years now? And, besides that, that's where Harriet Beecher Stowe's husband taught. Caleb, that is not just any college."

"Well, I left as soon as North Carolina seceded."

"And refused a commission with the North Carolina 26th Infantry."

Caleb reacted with surprise and started to speak, but Elizabeth cut him off.

"Oh yes, I do know, Caleb Cuthbait. Those officers love to chat away while I measure them for their pants and greatcoats. An officer, they say, and instead of accepting the commission, you enlist down here in the North Carolina 36th Coastal Artillery as a sergeant. And it's not because you were afraid of combat, for I heard what you did last month."

Caleb threw up his hands and stood. "Woman, I don't understand you. Before, you were upset I am in the Confederate military, fighting for what you say is the wrong side. Now, you seem upset that I'm not an officer. I think you just like to argue. I have to go."

Elizabeth Tuckerman rose from her chair and moved toward him.

"I know." She straightened the guns on his collar lapels. "Godspeed, Caleb, and may He protect you."

She kissed him. As he started to respond, she broke it off.

"Away with you. You are going to have to run the whole five miles or you will be late."

This was not how he had hoped the visit would end. His head spinning, he walked out the front door, turned left, and headed south. The Tuckerman cottage was just east of the winding Wilmington Road that twisted eighteen miles from the seaport of the same name on the east side of the Cape Fear River, down to the river's mouth. The sandy spit of land known by the North as Federal Point—and by the South as Confederate Point—slowly narrowed as it ran south, separating the Cape Fear River from the open Atlantic.

The eighteen miles were dotted with clusters of settlements of a few cottages, each one serviced by a wharf or landing. Captain Tuckerman's cottage, where his widow now lived, was five miles above the tip and one mile below Fort Fisher's supply depot, Sugar Loaf. Caleb had disembarked here after persuading the pilot of the small river steamer, bringing supplies to the fort, to let him off. The captain had obliged with a wink and an envious smile. Caleb had felt guilty about not seeing Elizabeth on his three-day pass, even before she raised the issue. He had hoped that a short visit might make amends.

The Wilmington Road was the only cleared route down the peninsula, and Caleb often ran on it for sport and exercise. And to get to the Tuckerman cottage. Today, as he ran—surprising deer, chickens, and settlers in turn—he recalled the amusement of his fellow soldiers, who hooted and hollered whenever they spied him running.

"There goes a horse!" one of them had yelled to boisterous laughter.

The storm of the last two days had subsided, the winds had died down, and the sky was clear. This was all bad news because, as pleasant as the weather was, it meant that the rumored Yankee fleet at Beaufort might sail. In Wilmington, people were convinced the fleet was heading farther south, to support Sherman. A second attack on Fort Fisher would wait until spring. If true, then this typical winter day in North Carolina was much more pleasant than the ones he had endured at Bowdoin.

Nothing grew well on the sandy peninsula, and he jogged past a steady landscape of struggling pine and scrub. Those who lived on the point were mostly river captains or others who survived on the river trade.

Approximately three miles north of the southern tip, Caleb reached the approach to the fort. As he did every time he entered, he marveled at its engineering. The structure was essentially L-shaped, with its strongest and most lethal fortifications situated in a line along its eastern edge, facing the open Atlantic. An enemy attempting to reach Wilmington by the Cape Fear River would have to sail past the batteries and round the point before steaming north to the seaport. As the last open port in the Confederacy, the route was swollen with blockade runners, supplying General Lee's Army of Northern Virginia.

At the northern edge of Fort Fisher's seaface wall, the peninsula narrowed to a half mile. It was here that the L swung left, as the fort sported a heavily barricaded front across the peninsula that ran from the Atlantic to the Cape Fear River, designed to defend against a ground assault from the north.

This wall was called the landface. It was comprised of fifteen mounds of piled sand, each approximately thirty feet high and twenty-five feet wide. In military terms, these earthen mounds were called "traverses." The mounds were covered by wild grass, planted to prevent erosion.

Compared to the masonry forts of old, an earthen fort could more readily absorb an enemy's exploding shells. These rolling traverses also prevented an enemy shell wiping out a line of soldiers stationed across a more traditional level parapet.

In the dips between traverses, the landface still reached twenty feet in height. Each dip housed cannons, fortified by sandbags. During an attack, the wall would be lined with infantry.

Most cannons along the landface were giant Columbiads. In the middle of the landface, a tunnel, known as a sally port, connected the interior of the fort with a raised gun emplacement just outside the fort's wall. Field artillery pieces could be wheeled out through this sally port to target advancing infantry.

The space beneath the traverses had been hollowed out into giant rooms braced with lumber called "bombproofs." The soldiers would retreat to them during shelling. The bombproofs were connected by a tunnel that ran the length of the landface.

The first half mile north of the landface was cleared of trees to provide the defenders a clear line of fire. A wooden palisade nine feet high ran parallel with the landface to delay enemy infantry charging south. A minefield lay buried in the middle of the peninsula, just north of the landface.

The Wilmington Road entered the fort from the riverside across a marsh, or slough, at the open side of the north-facing fortification. A wooden bridge crossed the slough.

As Caleb approached the bridge, he slowed to a walk so as not to alarm the sentries. They recognized him, and he entered the fort without challenge. He walked along the remnants of the old road, away from the land-facing batteries. He was assigned to Mound Battery, located at the southern tip of the fort. From that spot northward, the Atlantic fortifications consisted of a line of high earthen works dotted with gun mounts. At the juncture, where the wall swung westward, a salient called the Northeast Bastion had been constructed. From this battery, fire could be directed out to sea, up the beach, and westward to direct fire against the fort's land wall itself, if worst came to worst.

The seaface was constructed like the landface, with its own bombproofs and connecting tunnel.

Just outside Mound Battery, Caleb paused and surveyed his duty station of the last three years. Mound Battery rose sixty-three feet above the ground, the highest point on the fort. Like the Northeast Bastion, it also commanded three directions. It could fire out to sea and also protect the entrance to the river itself. Although the isolated Battery Buchanan located at the tip of the peninsula provided additional coverage of the mouth, Mound Battery was by far the most powerful.

"Why, lookey who's back from a three-day pass."

Caleb laughed at the two soldiers, who had exited the mound and now walked toward him.

"You spend those three days with the wida' lady?" the second soldier asked.

Caleb shook his head. "With my parents."

CHAPTER 3

Federal Point, North Carolina

January 12, 1865

Late morning

Elizabeth watched through her front window as Caleb trotted down the Wilmington Road. After he disappeared from view, she stepped out onto her porch and waited, in the unlikely event that he might impulsively decide to return. When the road remained quiet and empty, she went back inside.

Her cottage had been built by her late husband before they married. It was one of the few two-story structures on the peninsula, befitting his stature as a successful captain. Entering from the porch brought her opposite the center staircase, which ascended to a second-floor foyer, flanked by two rooms. The first floor had a kitchen to the left of the staircase and a parlor and living room to the right. In the rear of the property, a lean-to stable provided shelter for Cicero—her chestnut mare with the white star on its forehead.

Crossing to a peg on the far wall in her kitchen, she grabbed her late husband's coat and wrapped it around herself. She contemplated adding another log to the fire but was concerned that a hot flame risked her chimney flue. She would have to be quick.

She slid out the back door at the rear of the kitchen. She didn't follow Caleb's path to the road. Rather, she swung around the stable to a sandy trail that cut through the scrub and pine, one mile across the peninsula, to the open Atlantic. She didn't head straight toward the beach but, instead, angled northward. She wanted to come out above Battery Gatlin, the northernmost isolated battery that made up part of the rebels' Cape Fear Defense System. The battery had been abandoned after the December attack by the Union. It had fallen quickly then and was now considered indefensible. Still, one could never be too sure.

Despite her staged whining to Caleb, she was thankful he had not spent his three-day pass with her. Most passes issued by Colonel William Lamb, the fort's commander, were overnight passes for a rowdy night of drinking and whoring in Wilmington. She would have loved to have just spent three nights with Caleb—feeling his warm and gentle touch, wrapped in his supporting arms, so different from her late husband's. But there wasn't time for that. Not now.

She had no watch of her own, and Captain Tuckerman's pocket watch had long since stopped working. She had the money for a repair, if only she could locate parts in the war-ravaged Southern economy. Her sole timepiece was the mantel clock her parents had sent down from Hazardville and, as she hurried along, she knew she was late.

When she had first arrived, the peninsula had been called Federal Point. No one had objected to the name—especially since it was federal funds that had paid for the lighthouse and its operation at the peninsula's tip—but since war had come, the locals had renamed it Confederate Point. As Colonel Lamb had overseen the expansion of fortifications, the lighthouse had been torn down. Now, a beacon sat atop Mound Battery, where Caleb served as a captain of the gun. While the lighthouse had guided merchant shipping to the mouth of the Cape Fear River and its avenue to Wilmington, the new beacon was designed for the blockade runners who snuck up the river on moonless nights with munitions and other provisions in aid of the rebellion.

Elizabeth quickened her pace, stopping occasionally to listen to be sure no one else was about on this winter day.

As she crested the last dune, she surveyed the roiling Atlantic that stretched before her. On days after a storm, it was always rough. Today, it was also empty, save for the chilling onshore breeze that greeted her as she stood exposed. She pulled the oversized coat tighter. There, about fifty yards up the beach, she spotted Sara pacing away from her. Elizabeth was relieved to be in time. She knew better than to call out but, instead, hurried after Sara.

Perhaps sensing the approach of the older woman, Sara turned. She did not give her usual welcoming smile, and in a momentary panic, Elizabeth searched the scrub and sand to see if anyone lurked. Seeing nothing, she continued toward the eighteen-year-old.

The daughter of escaped slaves, Sara had been born in Philadelphia. Educated in a Quaker school in the Germantown section of that city, she could read and write, and she spoke as well as any educated white woman Elizabeth had ever met.

"Are you alright?" Elizabeth asked as she approached.

The young woman nodded. "They've sailed."

Elizabeth stopped in her tracks. "How do you know? Did someone tell you?"

The young woman shook her head. "No. It's in the Northern papers. *The Philadelphia Inquirer* reported that transports left Hampton Roads six days ago—destination Fort Fisher. Miss Emma has a friend at New Bern who said a reporter at the *Baltimore American* also had the story, but the White House threatened to arrest him if he printed it. I imagine the fleet will leave Beaufort any day now, if they haven't already."

"You were just there," Elizabeth protested. She spun to face the open water and carefully searched the horizon for any sign of the federal fleet. Seeing none, she turned back.

"They couldn't have left yet," Elizabeth said. "They would be here."

Sara was adamant. "I was in Beaufort two days ago and met with the admiral's own captain. I gave him your last information. The port was busy with loading, and the number of ships at anchor was increasing. There were troopships, but the rumor was Georgia. More ships than usual," she added with a confident smirk.

Elizabeth was stunned. There was nothing on the street in Wilmington. If Sara Carter knew the transports had sailed from an article in a Philadelphia newspaper, how could it be that the rebels in Wilmington or at Fort Fisher didn't know? Caleb had said nothing, and if the rebels were expecting an imminent attack, Colonel Lamb would never have given his best sergeant a three-day pass.

None of her seamstress clients, with their demand for new uniforms and greatcoats, had any inkling, of that she was quite sure. And Caleb would not have stopped in on his way back if he had been summoned to return.

"Two days ago?" Elizabeth asked.

Sara nodded. "I've been on the road for two days with Miss Emma. Even with your letter of passage, we took side paths and stayed off the main roads when we could. Not easy to do with a cart."

"I've got to think," Elizabeth said. Spreading the back of her late husband's coat as a cushion, she plunked down on the sand facing seaward. Even in the darkest days with her husband, she had so enjoyed sitting on this Carolina sand, sometimes staring peacefully at the water for what seemed like hours. But there was no peace now.

She had carefully forged a letter of passage for Sara, who posed as a housemaid for a fictional mistress who had traveled to New Bern and taken ill, just north of Jacksonville, North Carolina. New Bern had been in federal hands since '62, so there was no way for a curious rebel sentry to check Sara's fictional story. Sara traveled with Emma Lonergen, a white Wilmington housewife, who posed as Sara's owner's sister, accompanying the slave back and forth to New Bern.

Like Elizabeth, Emma and her husband were members of Wilmington's clandestine Loyal Union League, a shadowy group of Wilmington citizens who supported the Union and who engaged in, among other services, spying for the federals. Just prior to the Christmas attack, Emma Lonergen had written an anonymous letter to General Bragg, the area's Confederate commander with jurisdiction over the fort, reporting that personnel at the fort had agreed to spike their cannons and surrender at the first approach of Union warships. The intention had been an attempt to generate mutual distrust and suspicion and perhaps force a change in command just before the attack. However, the plan failed when the letter was passed on to Colonel Lamb, who dismissed it out of hand as an obvious hoax.

Elizabeth served as the league's informal president. As concerned as the rebels were with uncovering the activist group, her status as a widow had kept them from suspecting her. George Washington had used women as spies and couriers during the Revolution, and their gender had allowed them to pass unmolested through British lines. The rebels had learned little from the British mistake.

In reality, Sara and Emma never went to New Bern. Once above rebel lines, they would swing east toward Beaufort, the headquarters for the Union's North Atlantic Blockading Squadron. There, along with other spies, they passed along information about fortifications, troop movements, and munitions to the Yankee navy.

"Does he want to meet with me this time?" Elizabeth asked.

Sara shook her head and joined her on the sand. Last fall, after General Godfrey Weitzel was named to lead the Union ground forces in the Christmas attack, he had sailed down the North Carolina coast to reconnoiter the area. Elizabeth had been ferried aboard his ship as it lay offshore. She reviewed maps and plans of the area with the general, telling him, in no uncertain terms, that she knew every pine and scrub between Wilmington and the New Inlet, which formed the northern entry to the Cape Fear River, just above Smith Island in the river's mouth. She assured General Weitzel that the force at the fort was depleted. Half of the garrison's complement of men had been sent west to bolster the efforts to stop Sherman in Georgia. Another fifteen hundred rebel soldiers had been taken from surrounding units. There were now fewer than eight hundred untrained and generally untested soldiers at the fort. Morale and munitions were running low.

General Weitzel had appeared impressed with the information. As Elizabeth had been rowed ashore after her meeting, she was buoyed with confidence of a coming Union success. But General Benjamin Butler, Weitzel's regional commander, had decided to accompany the force, and as the highest ranking officer in the expedition, Butler had assumed command. Weitzel had stayed on and had gone ashore with the partial force Butler had chosen to land. Elizabeth met with him onshore, bringing him within a few hundred yards of the western edge of the fort's landface, and had pleaded with him that her information was accurate. Again, she thought she was successful, but Butler ordered a withdrawal without ever mounting a ground assault against the fort, despite two days of naval shelling. The Christmas attack had ended in failure.

"There is no request to meet with you, or anyone else, this time, although General Butler won't lead this attack," Sara said. "He's been 'retired.'"

"I understand," Elizabeth responded. She tried not to show her frustration at the federal officers' stubbornness. She wondered what else she could try.

"Go back to Wilmington," she said, perking up, "and you and Emma make your way back to Beaufort. Leave tonight if possible. Perhaps the gunboats have not yet sailed. Tell them that Bragg is still having some sort of military parade event in Wilmington for Hoke's men. They are being sent north to attack New Bern. Military balls have been scheduled. Bragg is not prepared to move, and several of his officers believe that, in the event of a naval attack, he will take up a defensive line, as he did at Christmas. His own men doubt he will move against the federal army. He will do everything he can to protect Wilmington and won't risk a counterattack. If the federals will only wait a few days, maybe a week, Hoke's men will be gone from Wilmington and engaged."

"This is what I just told them," Sara complained. "You want us to risk going back on the road to tell them again? No doubt, by now the fleet has sailed."

Rather than answer, Elizabeth stared out at the open ocean. She was asking a lot of this eighteen-year-old girl, not to mention of Emma Lonergen.

"And isn't that just what all junior officers would say to a woman about their superiors?" Sara pressed.

It was Elizabeth's turn to be adamant. "That is not what the officers say about Lamb, no matter how much I cajole them. They feel the same way about General Whiting too. But no one thinks Bragg will move against a landing army. If we say it enough times, perhaps someone up north will finally listen."

Sara stood up. "There is still daylight. I'll head back to town. I can make Wilmington by nightfall, and we'll set out in the morning. Although," she added mischievously, "I don't think Mister Lonergen will be too pleased. He's concerned that his neighbors are starting to get suspicious about all of Emma's travels to New Bern."

Elizabeth rose to her feet and tightly hugged the young woman. For the second time that day, she offered a sincere Godspeed and His protection to someone very dear to her.

CHAPTER 4

USS Iosco

January 12, 1865

Early Afternoon

A cold mist struck Patrick Sheedy's face as he climbed onto the deck of the *Iosco*. It was the first time he had seen light that day, and he paused to allow his eyes to adjust. Next to him, Seamus Flanagan did the same.

"You think we're in trouble?" Patrick asked.

Seamus gestured at the sea around them. The *Iosco* was in one of two battle lines of gunboats and ironclads steaming south. Between the battle lines was a line of transports containing the nine thousand soldiers.

Seamus let out a low whistle. "I'll tell you, laddie, this time we have the shot."

Captain John Guest stood amidships, speaking with his helmsman. The pair worked their way back through the clutter toward the raised deck. Sailors adjusted lines and stowed gear. Powder monkeys, some as young as fourteen, scrambled past, carrying boxes of powder and shells to the guns. They were hurrying. Everyone was moving quicker than usual. "Battle speed," the men called it.

We're getting ready, Patrick thought grimly as he dodged a powder monkey straining under a box of powder larger than himself and took in the scene of controlled frenzy.

The *Iosco*, a Sassacus-class "double-ender" steam gunboat, was built for one purpose only: patrolling the narrow inland waterways. Constructed at the Larrabee and Allen shipyard in Bath, Maine, she was the second ship of that class. Launched in March of 1864, the *Iosco* was commissioned a month later. With an eleven-hundred-seventy-three-ton displacement, and just slightly over two hundred feet in length, the wooden ship was thirty-five feet across and drew a little over eleven feet fully loaded. She was a coal-fired, steam-driven, side-paddle wheeler with a low target profile.

But it was her armaments that set the Sassacus class apart. The *Iosco* was equipped with two one-hundred-pound Parrott Rifles, four nine-inch Dahlgren smoothbores, two twenty-four-pound howitzers, one heavy twelve-pounder, and a regular twelve-pounder. With both boilers firing, she could make nine knots.

At the ladder leading to the raised helm deck, the pair paused and waited for the sentry to allow them to pass. When the marine looked up, the captain nodded. Patrick followed Seamus up the iron rungs.

Instead of addressing the two men, Captain Guest finished his conversation with his helmsman and then motioned for them to follow. The captain led them back into the bowels of the ship to his personal cabin. Neither had been there before.

Once inside, Captain Guest sat on a stool and faced the men. There was no extra seating, so they remained standing. Even had there been chairs, they would not have sat in his presence.

"Flanagan, is it?" the captain began.

"Aye, Captain."

"And Landsman Sheedy?" the captain asked, turning to Patrick.

"Aye."

"How old are you, Landsman?"

"Twenty-two, sir."

"And you?" he asked, turning back to Seamus.

"Twenty-eight, sir."

The captain paused, and Patrick got the distinct impression that he was struggling for the right words. It surprised him, for the captain generally exuded a confident manner and commanding presence. Since shipping aboard, Patrick had never had so much as a direct word with the captain, and now he had been invited to his cabin. He shifted uncomfortably.

As if noticing the motion, the captain looked directly at the landsman.

"You shipped in Boston, Landsman. Last June?"

"Aye."

"You have been with us since your enlistment, since we put together the crew in New York, is it not?"

"Aye."

The captain nodded and turned his attention back to Seamus.

"And you, Seaman, you've been in the navy since '61. And three years on merchant sailing ships before that."

It was not a question, but a statement, and Seamus Flanagan did not answer.

After a pause, the captain continued. "It's been a long war, gentlemen, no matter how long each of you has been in. And the men seem to like you, like both of you, leastways that is what I hear from my officers. That's important in this navy."

The captain cleared his throat and straightened. "Gentlemen, for almost four years, two large armies have slugged this war out. In the east, the armies have clashed in Virginia, Maryland, and even Pennsylvania. Clashed, buried their dead, and disengaged. One side or the other claims that they won this battle or that, but at the end of the day, little changes. No great capital is taken. Richmond and Washington both stand today as they did when President Lincoln took office. Both sides continue to pour men and materiel into hell's fury.

"And we, here in the navy, our job has been to shut down the South's supplies. We all know, gentlemen, that not much gets manufactured in the South. The rebels' army stays alive as long as it can sell cotton and buy powder, shot, supplies, food—everything it needs—in Europe, and we have been tasked since '61 with blockading the rebels. With shutting down their resupply routes.

"And we've done a good job," the captain continued. "Of the eleven major ports they had when this war began, we have successfully block-aded, captured, and closed ten. Only one remains open, here in North Carolina—men and munitions sailing up the Cape Fear River to Wil-mington and then overland to Robert E. Lee's Army of Northern Virginia. We can't take Wilmington by land, and we can't choke off its access to the Atlantic by the Cape Fear River until we take that damn fort that guards the mouth. Take Fort Fisher and we close the river, shut down

Wilmington, and Robert E. Lee and his band of rebels will run out of supplies in a matter of months."

"Begging the captain's pardon," Seamus said, clearing his throat, "but we tried, sir. The Good Lord knows we tried."

Captain Guest nodded. "That we did. We gave it to Johnny Reb for two days at Christmas, but the troops . . ." He let his voice trail off.

"But no matter," the captain resumed, regaining his composure. "We will try again, and this time we will take it. And that will be the end that sends us all on the way home."

"Captain, some of the men say—" Patrick began.

"I know what the men say, Seaman, but I say it can and will be taken," the captain continued firmly. "There's a new commander in charge of the army forces now, Major General Terry, and he's been told to be aggressive. He'll have nine thousand regular army troops."

The captain hesitated, and Patrick watched him draw a deep breath. "And he's to have another thousand men from the boats, marines and sailors."

"So, it be true, then?" Patrick asked. "The rumor?"

Captain Guest looked sharply at the landsman. "Scuttlebutt travels fast in this navy, Landsman."

"Aye, Captain, but—"

"No buts, Landsman. We will take it."

"Captain, sir," Seamus interjected. "As you say, sir, I've been in ships six years—three in the merchants and now three in this navy. We are not trained fighting men. Trained in the afternoon drills to repel boarders, yes, or board a blockade runner with pistols and cutlasses, aye, we can do that, but we are not an army to march into battle."

"I know that, Seaman."

"Well then, begging the captain's pardon again, but the army has a system in place. They have colonels to give commands to majors, who give orders all the way down to sergeants and corporals in charge of small groups of men. They have flags to show where each unit is supposed to be. Captain, no thousand men in this flotilla know each other beyond their shipmates. A thousand men landed on the beach under the fort, under *that* fort, Captain, all running around and no one in command . . ."

Seamus's voice trailed off under the captain's stare. The seaman took a half step back.

"Aye, Captain."

"Those are our orders, and Admiral Porter has asked for volunteers from all the ships to land ashore. We will fight under the command of Fleet Captain Breese."

"And who will lead the men from this ship, let alone the thousand?" Seamus asked. "Are we to elect a sergeant to work the men, or will we all try to listen to Fleet Captain Breese at once?"

Instead of answering, the captain stood and looked each man in the eye. Patrick swallowed hard.

"As I said, the men respect you two. The admiral has asked for volunteers, but they will need leaders. Yes, we'll have ensigns, but as you say, Seaman, we need sergeants, someone the *Iosco's* men will trust. Overall command of the sailors will fall to Captain Breese. But within the thousand, I would like you two to keep the *Iosco's* men together, keep them calm, and make sure they do their duty. Ensigns Jameson and Feilberg will go ashore and provide overall command of our sailors, and I have told them to ask who wants to go from the *Iosco*, but I need you two."

"And if I may ask, Captain, what are us able seamen and landsmen to fight with?" Seamus asked.

The captain almost smiled. "As you said, you have all been trained in repelling boarders with revolvers and cutlasses. We have plenty aboard. You will use them to take Fort Fisher. You are to meet with the ensigns on the forward deck after evening meal. We will be arriving off Federal Point tonight. We begin the bombardment at first light, and the troops will land shortly after. You may not go ashore right away, but Admiral Porter has committed to the plan. That is all."

The pair saluted awkwardly in the tiny space and backed out of the cabin. They didn't speak until after they made their way back up to the deck.

"It's madness," Patrick said when he was sure they were alone. "It's like Jeremiah Phillips said, no one here joined up to fight. And I didn't volunteer to go ashore and battle cannons with a cutlass."

"Then I'll ask you the same question I asked Mister Phillips this morning, laddie boy," Seamus said, "why'd you join up? Prize money, like Mister Vranken?"

The pair continued toward the bow. James Morris, the contraband who had risen to the position in command of the ship's howitzer, was inspecting its barrel. His crew fetched cleaning rods and solvents as he barked orders. Morris was one of the four Negroes on the *Iosco* who was not a coal heaver.

"I'm not like him," Patrick said, gesturing toward the gun. "James Morris is going to love firing that thing at Fort Fisher, killing as many Southern soldiers as he can with every salvo. I've seen his motivation. It's written in the scars across his back. But I'm not like him."

"No?" Seamus asked.

Around them, the flotilla continued to plunge toward the winter sun that sat low on the southern horizon. They were still heading south, and as the sun moved to the west, the ships would turn with it and begin their approach to the Cape Fear River and its protectorate fort.

"Then why?" Seamus asked.

"It was this or the army," Patrick answered. "I was about to get drafted. They found my name when I was living in Brooklyn and caught me up in Boston. Seamus, I've only been in this country five years. That's a bit wee of a time to die for it, don't you think?"

At the bow, Seamus turned and leaned his elbows back against the rail.

"So, you don't think you're like him?" he asked, gesturing back at the contraband inspecting the boxes of gunpowder the powder monkeys were dropping at his feet. "When did you say you came over?"

"Fifty-nine. I had just turned seventeen."

"With your parents, right? From Mitchelstown, in County Cork?"

"Aye."

"And tell me, lad, again, why'd you come?" Seamus asked.

"What?" Patrick asked. "You know damn well why I came, why we all did. Seamus, you came over, what, maybe five years before me? Why would you even ask? My grandfather was at Vinegar Hill. Between the landlords and the sheriffs and the redcoats, where were we to go? But I didn't expect to come to the middle of a war and then be asked—no, then be told—to fight in it."

Seamus nodded. Reaching into his pocket, he extracted a knife and a plug of tobacco. When Patrick shook off his offer, Seamus cut himself a slice and began chewing.

"You didn't think you were coming to a war," he said. He turned and spit over the side. "Well, I guess none of us did. But think of this war, laddie. Why is this government fighting it? This was not some war started when folks who could not take it any longer rose up with pitchforks. This was no American Revolution, fighting against the English. Or French peasants overthrowing an oppressive king."

Seamus turned back to Patrick, eyes blazing. "No. This was the government itself that started this, that made a decision to fight and sacrifice. Now why? Was it because the Negro had so much power and influence over the men in Washington? You know as well as I do, me boy, they did not. This government, this country, decided to fight for people who had no power, no influence, no gold, no riches. Thousands of men have died, laddie, been torn apart and slaughtered at Antietam and Vicksburg and Gettysburg, so that the Negro could be free. So that no one will own him and whip him and treat him like the English treat us. They did that for the Negro, for God's sakes.

"And, laddie," Seamus continued, moving off the rail toward Patrick, "if a government would do that for the lowliest Negro, then that's a government that could do it for Catholics or the Jew or Irish. Simply because it is right. It is this government that did this, laddie, and that is why I joined. So if they need me to battle cannons with a cutlass, then that is what I will do.

"But maybe," he added, stepping back and winking, "we can wrangle ourselves a pair of revolvers."

CHAPTER 5

Fort Fisher

January 12, 1865

Midafternoon

Sergeant Caleb Cuthbait peered across the open ocean through his field binoculars. He always enjoyed the view from atop Mound Battery. To the north, he could see up the Carolina coast, even as it bent eastward. And in the mornings, the direct sunrises could be spectacular.

Behind him, his gun crew waited patiently.

"Again," he said.

He turned to face them as they began yet another "dry practice" of wheeling the ten-inch Columbiad around, swabbing the barrel, and then pretending to load powder and shot down the muzzle. Live fire was more valuable, but the fort couldn't afford to waste munitions. There were perhaps three thousand rounds left in the garrison, and they needed to be husbanded carefully.

"Wait!" he barked.

It was not his whole crew that he worried about, but rather its one new member. With so many of North Carolina's men away fighting, or dead, the Confederacy had begun to rely on auxiliary units known as the "Junior Reserves." The men derisively called them the "seventeen-year-olds," and one had just been assigned to Mound Battery.

"Virgil, is it?" Caleb asked. He doubted the boy was even seventeen.

The youngster drew himself full up and barked a "Yes, sir!"

The men snickered. Caleb silenced them with a glare and stepped toward the youngster. "Peydreau?"

"Yes, sir! Private Virgil Peydreau, sir."

"Well, Private, first of all, I'm not an officer, so there is no need to call me sir. In fact," Caleb said, looking over the rear parapet to the parade ground behind the seaface, "calling me that in front of those who *are* officers around here might set them on edge a little bit, if you know what I mean."

"Yes, sir," Virgil began, then stammered when the other men again chuckled. "Sorry . . . eh, what should I call you then?"

"Well, you can call me Sergeant, or you can call me Caleb, but truth is, Virgil, when things start getting busy around here, we won't really have time to call each other anything."

"You mean, the Yankees?" Virgil scoffed. "Why those Yankees ain't coming back here, not if they know what's good for them. We done kick their behinds all the way back to Washington."

Virgil turned back, nodded at the other crew, and dramatically spit off the parapet. "That's what I think of them Yankees. Bunch of yellow-bellied cowards that are too afraid to ever come back."

"Well," Caleb shrugged, "perhaps you should get yourself a spot on General Bragg's inner circle in Wilmington. He apparently shares your belief that they're not coming back. Leastways, not until the spring," Caleb finished, raising his binoculars back to the ocean.

"Why, I ain't afraid of no Yankee," Virgil continued behind him. "They can dig up any old Yankee they want, the biggest Yankee of all, Abe Lincoln himself even, and if he were here, why I'd plunk him in the rear end with a Minié ball, that's what I'd do, yes, sir."

Caleb lowered his binoculars and turned back to his men. "Well then, Private Peydreau, you might as well learn how to use this cannon correctly, so you can give your ass-plunking to some Yankee without killing yourself.

"Lookey here," Caleb continued. He grabbed the ramrod from its mount on the side of the Columbiad's carriage and held it out in front of Private Peydreau.

"This ramrod has two ends. One is an iron plug, and this," Caleb gestured, turning the rod upside down, "is the sponge end."

Caleb pointed with his toe at the leather bucket at his feet. "When the time comes, this bucket will be filled with water. Never fire the cannon, gentlemen, unless this bucket is filled. The Columbiad is a ten-inch smoothbore cannon, capable of sending a one-hundred-twenty-pound iron projectile over forty-eight hundred yards. That's almost three miles. After it fires, it is very hot inside the barrel. *Very* hot."

Using the ramrod, Caleb pointed at the wheeled carriage on which the behemoth sat. The carriage rested on a set of slightly inclined rails.

"After discharge, the momentum of the blast will roll it backwards. But the incline will stop the roll. As you can further see, the carriage itself is positioned on this circular traversing rail, which allows it to be turned.

"And after you fire it," Caleb continued, "swing this carriage all the way around so that the mouth faces away from the enemy. Despite what you may witness at your town's parade days, never service a cannon with the mouth pointing at the enemy. That will put you in their line of fire and more than likely get you killed."

Caleb reached out to the carriage. Instantly, his crew followed suit, and together they swung the Columbiad's mouth farther away from the sea until the cannon pointed almost straight up the coast.

"Remember how hot the barrel will be," Caleb continued. "If you wedge powder down a hot barrel, maybe one that even has fires still flickering inside, why, that will ignite the powder, and the ramrod will become its own cannonball, probably taking a man's arm, or worse, with it."

Caleb dipped the sponge end into the empty bucket. "After you've got it turned away from the enemy, use the soaked end to sponge the whole barrel to cool it down, and make sure that any embers inside are out. Only then should you insert the powder and," Caleb turned the rod over, "tamp it in with this end. If everything is fine, then drop in the projectile, shot or grape, whatever we're using, and then gently tamp that in as well."

Pointing at the other cannons atop the Mound Battery, Caleb added, "And it's the same drill for these rifled thirty-two-pounders."

"Grape? This is a sea-facing cannon. Why would we use grape against ships?" Virgil asked with the wide-eyed wonder of youth.

Caleb nodded and returned the ramrod to its hook. "That's a good question, Virgil. You see, despite what you and General Bragg may agree upon, I think the Yankees will be back long before spring. Long before."

He pointed up the coast. "And when they do, they'll land up that peninsula—oh, four or five miles up, just out of range of our guns. And after they get a force together, they may not be as yellow as y'all think. Indeed, they'll come down here in force, thousands of them. And this will be after their ships have rained shot and shell on that land wall, and we'll need every cannon we have, including this one, turned north to try and stop them."

At the approach of Lieutenant Daniel Pinson, Sergeant Cuthbait instructed his men to oil and lubricate the carriage wheels before wordlessly moving off with his superior officer. Pinson led him down the ladder to the parade ground, filled with wooden barracks at the rear of the seawall.

"Any news?" Caleb asked.

Lieutenant Pinson shook his head. "I thought you'd have some, just having been to Wilmington and all."

Around him, men strolled to and fro. A few had already started fires for the evening meal. The pair meandered their way through the encampment, occasionally greeting soldiers they recognized.

"It was a social visit," Caleb said. "I wasn't invited for lunch with General Bragg."

"Did you have a chance to visit Miss Belle's?" Pinson asked with a sly expression. "Down by the docks?"

Caleb blushed and suppressed a smile. "I was visiting my parents. I don't think they would have appreciated it if I had come home one night reeking of Miss Belle's."

"And I don't imagine the Riva' Wida' would have appreciated it either," Pinson said.

"No, I don't suppose she would have."

"Speaking of whom, I have to pay her a visit myself."

When Caleb paused in his walk and turned to the officer, Pinson reassured him with a hand wave.

"Oh, don't worry. I need a new greatcoat, and she does seem to be the only one with red flannel."

"I think she stockpiled a warehouse before the war," Caleb sighed.

The lieutenant laughed. "Perhaps."

Their walk brought them to the riverbank. Pinson turned and faced his sergeant. His tone grew more serious.

"So, are we ready?" he asked.

Caleb hesitated. He tried to choose his words carefully.

"The fort is ready, sir, but . . ."

"Yes?"

Caleb swept his hand. "The fort is impressive. The armament, the design, the traverses between gun mounts to absorb exploding Yankee shells, the underground bombproofs for the men to take cover in—those aspects are impressive. Colonel Lamb has done an incredible job restructuring this fort over the last two-and-a-half years since he's taken command. Everything has been built up and improved."

"But?" Pinson asked patiently.

Caleb took a deep breath. "First of all, it's the men. Oh, they're good men, but we don't have nearly enough. We can withstand a shelling from the Yankees, but a land assault will involve thousands of soldiers, most probably veterans from the Petersburg campaign. We have what, eight hundred men here?"

"That's what General Bragg is for," Pinson said. "He's up in Wilmington, less than twenty miles away. He's got General Hoke's division under his command. He can send men down the river by steamboat when we need them. And he can come down the peninsula and trap the Yankees between himself and the fort."

"I still don't like it." Caleb shook his head. Perhaps it was better not to choose his words so carefully. He nodded toward the river.

"Look, in December, we had a telegraph line strung along this side of the river up to Wilmington. Why, the first thing that Butler's men did when they landed was cut it. We need to communicate with Wilmington if we are going to get help from Bragg."

"We learned our lesson," Pinson said. "The line now runs underground from the seaface to the river, then under the river to the west side, and then up along that side of the river to Wilmington."

"Sure," Caleb exclaimed, "but that's just it. The telegraph station is on the seaface, facing the enemy's gunboats. If their bombardment hits that . . ."

"Then we'll signal across the river to a telegraph operator to tap out a message," Pinson finished.

"Or we could just move the station to the river's edge, away from the seaface," Caleb argued.

"Too exposed," Pinson said. "Anything else?"

Caleb pointed at the landface and resumed walking north, along the river's edge.

"The west end of the wall," he said. "I walked down the Wilmington Road right into the fort through the area where the wall stops."

"It's marshy," Pinson said. "Tough to cross. Even for Yankees."

"With a wooden bridge across the marsh that the blues will run across unless . . ."

"Unless?" Pinson pressed.

"Unless we wire it and blow it up as soon as they land," Caleb finished.

He stopped and took his lieutenant by the arm. "The fort is good," he said earnestly, "but there are so many weak points. Especially the men. We just need more, and when the time comes, telegraph or not, I don't know if we can get General Bragg down here to help us."

CHAPTER 6

USS Iosco

January 12, 1865

Late afternoon

The foredeck was crowded. Including himself and two officers—Ensigns Jameson and Feilberg—Patrick Sheedy counted forty-three men. The ensigns had spoken with nearly every sailor who would not be needed when the bombardment began. A few others, such as Nat Davis, had also tried to volunteer but had been rejected for various reasons. Nat would be needed in the boiler room on Andy Wilson's team.

Directly ahead of the bow, Patrick could make out the faint outline of land beneath the setting sun. The *Iosco* had slowed but still remained in battle formation behind the admiral's flagship, the *USS Malvern*. Soon the *Iosco* would branch off, and a new battle line parallel to the shore would form in anticipation of the bombardment. The fleet would anchor for the night out of the range of Fort Fisher's cannons. He wondered if the rebels entrenched behind the earthworks and heavy guns pointing seaward could see them yet.

Ensign Jameson appeared nervous. He held an Ames naval cutlass in his right hand—like the ones that the crew had trained with, which were stowed in volume in the locked armory below—and he was screeching that each man would be equipped with a cutlass and revolver and as much powder and ball as he could carry. The plan was to go ashore, aboard either the launch or cutter, and form up to the north of the fort after the bombardment had reduced its walls and guns to rubble. They were there only to support the army, Jameson stressed, so it was nothing their drills had not prepared them for.

Around Patrick, sailors wore various expressions. Many were sullen, keeping their thoughts to themselves. Boatswain Mate James Madison hummed, while Captain of the Hold John Barber whittled a piece of wood. Vranken and Phillips glowered, and Patrick wondered why they had volunteered.

Jameson rambled on about God and country, and the longer he continued, the more nervous he became. Patrick doubted whether he had ever spoken to as large a group.

Seamus wandered among the men, studying each sailor's face. Jameson was saying that the bombardment might last two or three days, and that sailors might not be put ashore until the bombardment had done its work. "A mop job," he said at one point. Yet, moments later, the ensign was saying that each man should be prepared to go ashore at first light.

Behind him, Patrick watched as the rest of the crew implemented the "clear the decks" order that Ensign Feilberg had given before proceeding to the bow. The forty-three volunteers had been exempted from the duty. It was a continuation of what Patrick had witnessed earlier that afternoon. Sailors gathered and stowed loose tools below. Lines were retightened and strengthened. Equipment that had been brought up for replacement was removed back below deck.

When the rebel shells started hitting the ships, it was not only their explosions that would kill and maim. Projectiles of loose articles would be propelled into men's bodies, ripping them apart. Chunks of decking—splinters, the men called them—would hurtle through the air, more deadly than any shot or Minié ball. The injuries they could inflict on tissue and bone would be as hideous as they would be catastrophic.

Sailors lifted sandbags from below and set them against the outside rails to block rifle fire. Others strung chain netting from the forward mast to retard chunks of deck or other debris that would be accelerated by exploding shells. Around the gun mounts, sailors constructed barricades of railroad ties, covered by heavy canvas, lashed to spikes driven into the decking. In the morning, men would carry their own hammocks and bedding topside and roll and lash them to the outside of the rail lines for additional protection.

But it was the appearance of the powder monkeys, lugging buckets of sand and water, that always unsettled the men. If a new crewman asked, he was quietly told that the water was for drinking during the fight, and the sand was to spread across the decks to absorb the rivers of blood that would flow and pool in spots. The decks would become so slippery that no man could cross them without falling.

And last, when all was stowed and lashed and the buckets positioned, Assistant Surgeon Kirk Bancroft and his medical mates would appear and construct a series of "cat lifts"—ropes and pulleys—at each hatchway so that the killed and maimed could be lowered during the fighting to the surgeon waiting to perform his grisly task below.

Ensign Jameson stopped talking, and now Ensign Feilberg addressed the sailors from a position in front of Patrick.

"It don't matter what the plan is," a voice whispered in his ear. Patrick swiveled to face Seamus, who had sidled up alongside him.

"When we land, laddie, the whole plan will go to the devil, leastways as far as us sailors go. We haven't trained for this. If the rebs attempt to board our spit of sand, why, I am sure we could repel them well enough. We know how to do that. But attack a fort, they say? What will matter on the morrow is that we keep the men together, and none of us go off on our own accounts."

As he spoke the last sentence, Seamus looked toward Jeremiah Phillips, who glared glumly at the new speaker.

Seamus moved in the direction of Phillips. Patrick followed along behind. When Seamus reached the sailor, he stood behind him and waited until there was a small clearing around Phillips before speaking softly.

"Jeremiah, me boy, it looks like you be going ashore for the captain's party."

The sailor turned. "As are you, Flanagan."

"Aye, and a tough one it may be. But you know, laddie, in order to survive this fight that's a-coming, we are going to need all of us pulling together, acting as if we are on the same side."

Seamus moved in close to the sailor, and Patrick leaned in to hear.

"Now I know that you are not the best of friends with Ensign Jameson—him being a pompous, educated sort of man—but I want you to know that no one should get any ideas ashore."

Phillips turned back toward Seamus and placed his hands on his hips. "So?" he challenged.

"Well, laddie," Seamus continued, "there'll be a heat of battle going on and much confusion, I say. Now, if during all this confusion, Ensign Jameson—or Feilberg for that matter—suddenly found himself shot in the back of the head, why, that would be one less man to protect all of us, and old Seamus here would not take too kindly to that. Do you hear what I'm saying, laddie?

"Oh," Seamus continued in a calm and even tone, "in case you were thinking that maybe in the din of battle something might happen to old Seamus first, well, laddie, I count six Micks on this here shore party, and we all have friends, including Patrick, and some of his friends be niggers."

Jeremiah Phillips blanched and then turned and wordlessly strode to the far side of the deck.

"I think he heard me," Seamus said to Patrick.

CHAPTER 7

Federal Point, North Carolina
January 12, 1865
Late afternoon—Early evening

Elizabeth watched Sara walk back up the beach and out of view, where she would find the waiting cart for the ride back up the Wilmington Road. Elizabeth retraced her steps across the scrub to her cottage. The fire still burned. After peeling off her coat and shoes, she sat before it, her feet extended to catch the warmth of its embers. When she had risen that morning, she had planned to saddle Cicero for a late-afternoon ride, but now she decided against it. She'd need the mare to be fresh.

So much was happening, and this time, so fast. At some level, she was annoyed that Sara was aware of the coming Union assault, while she had been left out of the circle of knowledge. General Weitzel had trusted her last fall. Even after General Butler assumed command of the Christmas attack, she had met with Weitzel on the peninsula during the assault and accompanied him along the river to within a few hundred yards of the fort. There they met Colonel Cyrus Comstock, the engineer, and Colonel Newton Curtis, whose New Yorkers hunkered, awaiting the order to charge.

But with just twenty-five-hundred of his sixty-five-hundred man assault force having landed on the peninsula, General Butler decided to withdraw. Curtis wanted to attack. Elizabeth and Colonels Curtis and Comstock had crouched in a rifle pit, and she pointed out which divisions remained at the fort and the strength and readiness of each. Curtis had dispatched messengers in an effort to sway Butler.

Elizabeth stayed at the front, convinced—with Colonel Curtis—that an order to attack would come forth. When yet another order to withdraw arrived, Curtis was furious, and Elizabeth was deeply disappointed. She consoled herself that at least Colonel Curtis had listened to her.

Now, she was unsure. The Northern newspapers that Sara obtained at New Bern reported that Congress, the president, Admiral Porter—hell, everybody—had been furious with Butler. At Porter's insistence, Butler had been replaced. Major General Terry, a former lawyer and court clerk from New Haven, in her home state, had been appointed to lead the army forces. But, for whatever reason, no one had contacted the Loyal Union League this time.

Well, that might change. If the Union forces at Beaufort were indeed loaded for Fisher, they might still need her, once ashore.

Impulsively, Elizabeth swung her feet off the footstool and dressed. Her pile of sewing beckoned, but if Sara was correct, there would soon be little need for rebel uniforms. Besides, she thought wryly, if she did fill her current orders, she might have difficulty getting paid—or spending the CSA scrip if she did.

The winter sun was slipping below the horizon. Darkness came quickly this time of year, but Elizabeth knew the peninsula well. She headed straight across the land, eschewing the northern route she had taken that afternoon.

She regretted her decision to send the young Negress back to Beaufort on short notice. Although Sara and Emma had mostly avoided sentries and pickets, each trip ran an additional risk for both whites and blacks.

She had first seen a Negro when she was a child. She was not sure of her exact age, but her younger sister Annie could walk and talk, and her brother Robert was starting to toddle.

At her family's tobacco farm in Hazardville, Connecticut, she and Annie had been hustled off upstairs to bed earlier than usual, without explanation. As they huddled under the blankets, there had been a knock at the door. It was tentative, but loud enough in the quiet home. The door opened, then quickly closed. Elizabeth thought it strange that she heard no words of greeting. She recognized hurried, whispered strings of conversations but could not discern most of the words.

At one point, a strange voice rose and addressed her father: "No one followed us, Rutherford, of that I am sure," followed by resumed whisperings. The door opened and closed again, and then all was silent.

In the morning, she had crept downstairs while Annie still slept. In the kitchen by the hearth, lying on his back on top of blankets and staring at her, was the largest man she had ever seen. He was black from head to toe.

Her mother shushed her from the room and back upstairs. Elizabeth reasoned that her father must have gone out early, for he was soon back, and for much of the rest of the morning, Rutherford Prescott and his wife, Molly, rushed about, casting nervous glances out the windows but speaking little. All the while, the black man sat by the fire, accepting food and drink, but saying nothing.

By the afternoon, he was gone, and her parents never spoke of the incident.

That was just the first. In the years that followed, the scenario repeated. Usually they arrived at night or, on rare occasions, in daylight, lying low in the back of a wagon. Sometimes it was a man, alone. Other times a woman or couple, and once she remembered a family. One man stayed for several months, and Rutherford put him to work with the other helpers on the Prescott farm. The Negro had lived openly in the workers' bunkhouse, but after a year, he too was gone.

When she was fifteen, Elizabeth was sent to the Mount Holyoke Female Seminary, just across the border in Massachusetts.

"I've taught you all I can at home," her mother said to her on the day she left, "but you and your sister have quick minds and need formal schooling."

Mount Holyoke was designed to train young women to become schoolteachers. The instructors were strict but fair, and Elizabeth learned history and read the classics. After a year, Annie joined her in the cloistered environment for young women. Both girls knew better than to mention the men and women who came in the night.

After finishing at Mount Holyoke, Elizabeth traveled one summer to visit her aunt and cousin in Baltimore. She intended to stay the season and return in the fall. It was there that she saw the peculiar institution firsthand—the slave markets, the public abuse, and the look in the eyes of those who had given up hope. She understood firsthand the night work that Rutherford and Molly performed.

After church one Sunday in Baltimore, she met Mister Frederick Tuckerman, the riverboat captain from Wilmington, North Carolina. He was older than she and possessed the air of a man who had seen a bit too much of the world. His full head of black hair, drooping mustache, Southern drawl, and irreverent manner attracted Elizabeth. There was a hint of danger about him, and it excited her.

Her parents wrote back immediately when they got her letter, commanding her to return to Hazardville. But by the time their letter arrived at her aunt's house, she was already Missus Frederick Tuckerman and on her way south to her new home on Federal Point.

It was only after arriving that she learned more about her husband. He was thirty-seven, not twenty-eight, and he drank heavily. And although he refused to talk about it, she learned that she might not have been the first Missus Tuckerman. Once, when he was away, she found a family Bible under an old blanket on a shelf in the shed. A bookplate inside identified it as the property of Frederick and Cora Tuckerman. When he returned and she asked about it, he struck her across the face, knocking her to the floor and drawing blood.

He stood over her, swaying and seething, and she could smell the alcohol and lechery that oozed from his pores.

"My past is mine only," he slurred before lurching away to his supper.

She learned to survive. His work required him to travel frequently, up the river to Wilmington and beyond, and he was often on the river for days at a time. This gave her the opportunity to read, not only those few books that she had brought with her from Baltimore, but also those she purchased in Wilmington with her seamstress money.

And it was good money. There were weeks where her success as a seamstress resulted in her bringing in more money than her husband, although she could never be sure if he made less that week or dropped it at a brothel. He never knew how popular a seamstress she had become, and over the years, she hid a sizeable sum, which he never found.

Her work also afforded her an excuse to go to Wilmington to measure clients, pick up supplies, or deliver product. She tried to schedule the trips when her husband was home. He never minded.

On one of these excursions, she met Emma Lonergen, long before war had broken out but at a time when it lurked precipitously on the horizon. Despite the image in the North, Southern states were not filled exclusively with radical fire-eaters. Many below the Mason-Dixon Line supported the Union and opposed slavery. And these were not just transplanted Northerners. Emma Lonergen and her husband were native North Carolinians.

Captain Tuckerman was not as generous in allowing her to travel out of state. Elizabeth never confided to her parents about her situation, but she knew they suspected. Their entreaties to come north for a visit forced her to pen countless excuses. She planned to save enough money to time one of her husband's multi-day trips with her own flight. With luck, she would be in Connecticut by the time he got back. Her one major contact with her parents occurred when they sent her the Waterbury chime clock that adorned her mantel.

But, for reasons she never understood, she stayed, even after she had hidden more than enough money.

As war drew nearer, she and Emma grew closer. After Lincoln's election in 1860 and North Carolina's secession, the social visits to the Lonergens became clandestine political meetings, and the meetings slowly evolved into planning sessions. When her husband was away, the Loyal Union League traveled down the peninsula to meet in her cottage, away from prying rebel eyes. They held a straw vote and elected Elizabeth president.

In the late summer and fall of 1862, yellow fever swept the Wilmington area, taking Captain Tuckerman with it. After his death, her role as the league's president expanded. It was in that capacity that she had met General Weitzel aboard his ship during his December scouting mission.

Now, as Elizabeth emerged from the scrub south of where she had met Sara, she hoped she could continue to be of service. The evening was turning chilly, although the sky remained clear. If Sara and the Northern press were right, and the fleet anchored in Beaufort was destined for Fort Fisher, it might have already sailed.

She scanned the horizon, searching for any hint that the fleet was en route. Her husband had owned a pair of field binoculars that she'd considered bringing with her, but a wandering rebel sentry might become suspicious seeing her staring out at sea with them, especially if it preceded an appearance by the federal navy.

Elizabeth was about to turn back to her cottage and supper when something caught her eye. It appeared like a low fog bank, isolated against the fading horizon. Then it grew larger and a bit darker. Just to its left, a second one appeared, darker than the first. Two ephemeral clouds on the horizon.

For a moment, Elizabeth assumed that the lighter cloud on the right was a blockade runner being pursued by a federal blockader burning darker coal. She studied the specters in an effort to ascertain if the darker one was gaining on the lighter. Soon, the lighter cloud would have to turn toward the coast and make a run for the Cape Fear River and the protection of the fort.

But the lighter cloud did not turn. At first, she thought the cloud was becoming darker, then she saw that a third wisp had appeared just to the rear of the lighter one. Then, a fourth appeared, followed quickly by a fifth. As the horizon became dotted with coal plumes, she was overcome with a sense of relief. She swiveled to the south and wondered if those standing guard atop the parapets knew what was approaching. Sara would not have to make that trip to Beaufort after all.

CHAPTER 8

Fort Fisher

January 12, 1865

Early evening

Caleb pulled the frying pan off the cook fire and examined the piece of pork his mother had given him when he left home that morning. Finding it satisfactory, he jostled the pan in the air, flipping the meat, and replaced the sizzling tin on the fire. He was so absorbed with his evening meal that he didn't hear the approach of one of the members of his gun crew.

"There's smoke," Corporal Jennings said.

Caleb looked up but did not grasp Jennings's meaning. He glanced back at his cook fire.

"On the horizon," the corporal explained.

"Runner?" Caleb asked, but already the corporal was shaking his head.

"Several plumes," he said earnestly.

Caleb studied the corporal's face. It was ashen. *It's time,* he thought.

Standing, he removed the pan and placed it on the sand. He kicked dirt on the fire until it was out. He started toward the battery before impulsively swinging toward his barracks. When he emerged, he had the binoculars his father had given him hanging around his neck. Upon seeing Caleb, the corporal turned and led the way to Mound Battery. As Caleb followed his corporal up the ladder, he wondered whether proper protocol dictated that he should climb first. Well, soon such things might not matter.

At the top, a handful of men stood at the parapet, studying the ocean. Caleb raised his glasses and counted eight plumes. Lowering them, he turned to his corporal.

"Go get Colonel Lamb," he said calmly. "Ask him to come up here, with my compliments."

When the corporal turned and descended the ladder, Caleb counted the plumes again. Still eight.

He looked around at a motley collection of soldiers. There was the posted sentry, two soldiers from the Signal Corps, and two others who had wandered up for the view. The sentry must have alerted the corporal, he reasoned.

Looking back down at the fort's interior, he noted men still sitting around cook fires or congregating in small groups. The checkerboards were out. Word had not yet reached them. He trained his glasses northward on the Northeast Bastion and saw motion. Men moved toward the parapet. He swung his glasses south, training them on the isolated Battery Buchanan, a mile south of the fort at the tip of Confederate Point. He could make out no movement and saw no one atop the mound. He frowned. Drinking again, no doubt.

Colonel Lamb ascended the ladder, followed by the corporal. Jennings must have found him on the parade ground. Proper deference there.

"What do you have, Sergeant?" the colonel asked as he approached. There was no need to answer. The plumes were merging into a low haze.

More men ascended the ladder. Caleb noticed Private Peydreau among them.

You're about to find out how yellow-bellied the Yankees are, my young friend, Caleb thought.

Colonel Lamb trained his own glasses on the horizon, no doubt attempting to perform the same estimate Caleb had. It was too early for an accurate ship count, but turning away was impossible for any of them.

"Go get the telegraph operator," Colonel Lamb said to no one in particular. "Send him to his station. I will be along shortly."

The order having been given to no one, no one moved. Caleb looked at one of the signal corpsmen and jerked his head toward the ladder. The man moved quickly, possibly glad to be away from a place that might soon become dangerous.

"I don't imagine there is any room for dispute," the colonel said calmly to Caleb. It was not a question so much as a wish.

The sergeant shook his head. "I am afraid not, sir. That smoke is getting heavy."

Colonel Lamb lowered his glasses and looked at the sky. "They've lost the light. They'll form up and anchor for the night. In the morning, they'll move in and . . ." There was no need to finish.

"I'll send a telegram to Wilmington," the colonel resumed. "You were just there, Sergeant. You think General Bragg will help us out?"

The sergeant in Caleb went to full alert. He chose his words carefully.

"I'm not sure, Colonel. The rumor had it that General Bragg was preparing to send Hoke north to attack the Yankees at New Bern. But they were still there when I left this morning. I think they were planning another military ball and parade," he added neutrally.

Colonel Lamb didn't react to Caleb's sarcasm. Perhaps he was intent on other things. Perhaps he agreed.

"Well, maybe I should send a second telegram, to your father then," Colonel Lamb said. "Ask for some prayers for us. Him being a preacher and all."

"I don't know," Caleb answered. "It's good to have God on our side, but I think I would just as soon have Hoke."

Behind him he heard one soldier react. "That's blasphemy!"

It was Private Peydreau.

Caleb half-turned to the youngster before nodding toward the approaching fleet. "Soon enough, Private, there will be blasts for all of us."

Despite the tension, Colonel Lamb laughed. "I'm glad you're keeping a sense of humor, Sergeant.

"Private!" Colonel Lamb bellowed to the remaining signal corpsman. "Do you have paper?"

When the soldier answered in the affirmative, Colonel Lamb dictated a telegram to General Bragg in Wilmington, informing him of the arrival of the Yankee fleet. He requested reinforcements for the fort and asked that Hoke's division be sent down the peninsula to contest the Yankee landing, which the colonel predicted would begin at first light.

After the private scurried down the ladder, Colonel Lamb turned back to Caleb. "Now we wait."

Caleb turned his attention back up the peninsula.

"Colonel," he began. "The Yankees will be landing three or four miles north of here and proceed south. Should you warn Missus Lamb? Perhaps, if she were across the river, she might be safer."

"Thank you, Sergeant, although it is not just Missus Lamb who might be in danger up the peninsula, eh?"

Caleb blushed.

The colonel dispatched a rider up the Wilmington Road to the Lamb cottage, directing his wife to pack herself and the children and be ready for immediate departure across the river. He instructed the rider to make sure his own barge at Craig's Landing was manned and ready to transport his wife and children out of harm's way. He then told the courier to continue up the road to the Tuckerman cottage and give a similar warning to the widow there.

"Now at least our women are safe, Sergeant," he said when the rider departed.

The colonel turned and climbed down the ladder.

Caleb continued to stare at the merging plumes of smoke as they slowly disappeared in the fading twilight. Then, with a start, he noticed that the Yankee ships had lit their signal lanterns. *Well, why not?* he reasoned. After all, it was not as if their movements were unexpected or especially secretive. And there was no Confederate Navy from whom they need hide.

Transfixed, he watched as the signal lamps rearranged themselves into battle lines outside of the range of the fort's cannons.

"Should we load the guns now, Sergeant?" Corporal Jennings nervously asked at his shoulder.

Caleb shook his head. "They won't approach until morning, and it might still rain tonight."

Behind him, he heard drummers begin to beat the long roll, the universal military call to battle stations. Caleb frowned. There would be no attack until first light. Better to let the men sleep, he reasoned, although there might be little of that this night. Well, at least rest, then.

As the men assembled on the parade ground, he heard officers shouting orders. Without looking back, he tried to calculate how many soldiers were left. The fort had been stripped of even more men after the failed Christmas attack, so confident was Bragg that the Yankees would not return until spring.

And if the Yankees had delayed even a few more days, Hoke's men would be gone north to New Bern, and there would have been no one to reinforce the garrison behind the walls and no one to trap the Yankees on the peninsula.

Caleb left his corporal on watch and descended the ladder. Though it was early, he went to his cot and lay down. To his surprise, he was awakened by Colonel Lamb's hand on his shoulder.

"You feel like going for a ride, Sergeant?" he asked.

When Caleb looked up quizzically, the colonel explained. "I haven't heard back from Craig's Landing. Nothing will happen around here till dawn. Perhaps we should take a ride to see our women."

The colonel's horse was already saddled, and his orderly bridled a second. Most of the fort's horses had been killed in the Christmas bombardment, and only a few had been replaced.

"When will you be back, sir?" the orderly asked. "What shall I tell Major Reilly?"

"As soon as I can," Colonel Lamb responded, swinging his leg over the saddle. "I will gladly risk my life, tomorrow, once I ensure that those I love are safe, tonight."

The pair rode quietly across the parade ground. The moon had risen, and Caleb calculated that it was after midnight. The frenzied activity that had erupted when the drummers had first beat the long roll had long since subsided. The guns on the seaward wall were lightly manned, and the watchers mostly stood about, counting the long lines of swaying signal lights that had settled out of range. Unassigned men had returned to their barracks to rest or sleep.

Caleb eased his mount back, allowing the colonel to lead through the riverside gate and across the wooden bridge that spanned the marsh. Once back on the Wilmington Road, he moved up alongside.

"You really don't think that Bragg will come," the colonel said as they walked along, cautiously guiding their mounts in the dim light. It was not asked as a question. When Caleb didn't answer immediately the colonel added, "I am not asking you this in front of the men."

"I don't know," Caleb answered truthfully. "If they were coming, they could already be here. General Bragg has such a reputation for bad luck."

Colonel Lamb snickered. "That's one way of phrasing it."

"I don't think he's afraid," Caleb quickly added. "The word in Wilmington was that he was preparing to send Hoke north to New Bern. That's not fear. And Hoke has good men, men who have been through a lot. General Bragg could just as easily send them down the peninsula to try and trap the Yankees on the beach."

"A classic hammer and anvil," Colonel Lamb said. "Or he could try and contest the Yankee landing itself, while the blues are still in their rowboats. But there is hesitancy in your voice, Sergeant."

Caleb took a deep breath. "General Bragg has to protect Wilmington. He may be afraid that, if he sends Hoke down and the counterattack goes badly, the Yankees will swing around him and capture an undefended Wilmington. In December, the word was that General Bragg had moved his own family out of town when the Yankees began landing here. He is concerned."

Colonel Lamb swore softly. "What the good general doesn't accept is, if he cannot save this fort, there is no saving Wilmington. If the Yankees take control of Confederate Point, they'll bring their transports around the tip and land on both sides of the river and march north. There will be nothing, *nothing* to stop them. They may land seven or eight thousand tomorrow to attack the fort. But if they take the fort, they could land another fifteen thousand, and Hoke will have no chance to stop them.

"It all comes down to this fort, Sergeant," the colonel concluded. "We know what happens if we lose the port. I wouldn't give Bob Lee three months after Wilmington falls before he runs out of everything. And once Lee surrenders, it's the end of the Confederacy. They'll hang Jeff Davis for treason, and any hope of Southern independence will be gone forever."

"I know," Caleb said.

"If we lose this fort, it won't matter if Hoke stands between the Yankees and Wilmington. Wilmington won't matter. The Yankees will just close the river from here. Bragg has to be made to see that. He *has* to send Hoke down."

To their left, Caleb heard the Cape Fear River as it washed toward the ocean. It did not appear that any steamers were out on the water that night. Soon, if things went badly, all river trade would be closed.

At the Lamb cottage, the two riders stopped. Colonel Lamb dismounted and entered the cottage while Caleb remained on his horse. There did not appear to be any activity within, and for a moment, Caleb assumed that Missus Lamb had already left with the children.

But then he heard the colonel's angry voice. "Damn it, Daisy! I sent a rider to tell you to pack, not ignore him. Now get up and let's pack!"

A moment later, the colonel reemerged, clearly frustrated.

"She went back to bed after the courier left," he explained sheepishly. "I'm going to get her packed and across the river. You ride ahead to your woman's cottage, Sergeant. I'll take care of things here. Bring her back with you if you choose. They can cross the river together."

Caleb thanked the colonel and wheeled his horse. As he rode out of the dooryard, he heard the colonel muttering, "Women!"

It was less than two miles to the Tuckerman cottage, and despite the darkness, Caleb found himself now trotting his mount. He assumed that he'd have to wake Elizabeth, and he wondered what her reaction would be when told of the approach of the federal fleet. When he arrived at the cottage, he pounded on the door. When there was no response, he opened it and went inside. The house was empty. She must have gotten word, he thought thankfully, and already fled to Wilmington for safety.

CHAPTER 9

USS Iosco

January 13, 1865

Friday morning

Although slightly longer than usual, Patrick's shift had gone quickly. He was thankful for that because he had lain awake in his hammock nearly all night.

By ten o'clock the previous evening, the *Iosco* had formed up in a battle line parallel with the shore. The Union ships had arrayed in three forward lines, with a fourth held to the rear in reserve. Captain Guest had ordered the boilers kept at half steam all night, and Patrick knew that his own earlier-than-usual shift would bring the boilers to full steam. The *Iosco* and her sister ships would creep in toward the shore, while maintaining a straight line, and commence pounding the fort. At the northern end of the battle line, some gunboats would cover the landing zone, which was planned one mile north of the site of the Christmas landing.

Patrick had been promoted from coal heaver to fireman on the *Iosco* in time for the Christmas attack—the Union's first attempt to take Fort Fisher. As the Union fleet had sailed away on December twenty-seventh, the fort had opened up with its cannons on the retreating armada as a final, if ineffectual, insult. Some Union sailors claimed they could hear the rebs jeering from the top of the parapets as the Union Navy sailed away.

The scuttlebutt was that General Butler had lost his nerve, and as the *Iosco* underwent repairs and resupply at Hampton Roads, rumors flew that Admiral Porter had begged General Grant to replace Butler. Whether the story was true, no one knew. Now Major General Alfred Terry would lead the ground forces. Take the fort, close down the South, and the war, which had gone on for four bloody years, would end.

Patrick had attempted to roll over in his hammock, always a tricky maneuver. All had been quiet below deck, but he knew that on the eve of battle few, if any, of the men were really sleeping. No one talked, for there was nothing to say, and talk about the looming battle would be viewed as both cowardice and a sure sign of bad luck. It would also invite sharp rebukes from those who feigned that it was disturbing their own sleep.

But at least, since he had first shift in the boilers, he would not be going ashore in the morning—that is, if Ensign Jameson was correct and the sailors were to join the army in the morning's first landing. If the sailor embarkation occurred after his shift, he would have no such excuse and would find himself being rowed ashore in one of the *Iosco's* launches. Then he would be on the beach, the same spit of sand he had seen in December from the bow as he watched the bombardment.

He had been in action before. After enlisting in Boston, he had joined the *Iosco* in New York as the ship assembled its first crew. From there the ship had sailed north, to protect shipping near the mouth of the St. Lawrence River and intercept blockade runners attempting to reach Halifax. They had rescued two other ships, one American and one British, but their deployment had otherwise been uneventful.

In November, they had captured the blockade runner *Sybil*, with its cargo of cotton—for which they were still owed prize money—and, of course, in December, he had been with the *Iosco* during the first attack on Fort Fisher. But no sailors had landed then, and the only battle damage had been a lucky shot severing the *Iosco's* foremast.

He worried how he'd behave onshore. The captain thought that the men respected and would follow him, but what would they follow him to? If he turned and ran, would they? What would the captain think then? Patrick didn't believe he was afraid to die, at least not more than anyone else, but what would he be dying for? For Seamus's grand view?

He wasn't sure if he ever fell asleep, but the boatswain's piping of all hands to stations jarred him. It was just after three o'clock a.m. Patrick rolled out of his hammock and dressed quietly. No one else spoke. By three thirty a.m., he and his two coal heavers were on duty in the boiler room.

They quickly brought the boilers to full steam, and at four o'clock, the gunboat weighed anchor and crept in at slow speed before again dropping anchor. His boiler room crew maintained enough steam in the event the *Iosco* had to move quickly. It did not.

At seven twenty a.m., the reverberating boom of the *Iosco's* howitzer shook the ship and, along with Sven and Nat, Patrick grabbed clean rags and stuffed them in his ears. The inside of the boiler room rang like the inside of a bell when the cannons fired.

Only the howitzer was firing, and the shots were spaced about two minutes apart. The ship was obviously not under attack, and Patrick could hear the distant booms of the other gunboats.

When his shift ended, he and Nat climbed up on deck while Sven headed to the mess for his midday meal. The pair worked their way to the bow, where other sailors had gathered.

The *Iosco* was not in front of Fort Fisher but anchored four miles north of the fort. To his left, two other Union lines of ships pounded the rebel fortifications. Closer in were the five ironclads. Many of the rebels' seaward-facing cannons had already been destroyed or knocked out. The defenders were firing back, but only sporadically. He discerned no damage to any of the Union ships, but he knew that any of them could still sustain devastating carnage.

Both of the *Iosco's* longboats were away, and Patrick watched as the launches ferried soldiers from the surrounding transports to the near shore. The rebels were not contesting the landing.

The *Iosco's* howitzer continued to fire, and Patrick watched as James Morris languidly gave orders to his gun crew. The crew took its time between shots, as did the other ships' gunners, and Patrick watched as the shells arced over the beach and dropped into the woods behind in preventative support of the landing.

"Maybe they'll be no ground attack, boss," Nat said next to him. "I be watching them ironclads. The *Monadnock* done got four hits in a row right in the middle of them reb bastards." The contraband chuckled. "Right in a row, boss. I don't think their parade ground be too smooth right now." He chuckled again, and it erupted into an almost gleeful laugh.

"I tell you, lad, them rebs don't give up that easily," Patrick said as he watched the fifth consecutive shot from the *Monadnock* hit the middle of the fort's seaside wall. "They all be dug in there like bugs in the earth, and when our boys attack, the grays'll come out and fight, all right.

"Say, who the devil *is* the *Monadnock's* gunner?" Patrick asked.

Nat turned to his fireman and flashed a wide, toothy smile.

"Why, that be old Joseph Jacobs himself. He done escape north when I did eight years ago, and we both signed ourselves up at the same time. Old Joseph, he done start out as a coal heaver like me, but he up and worked his way on to a gun crew, and his captain sure enough figure out that Joseph, he got the eye. You know what I mean, boss? He got himself the eye," Nat repeated reverently, turning his attention back to the fort before spitting over the rail. "I wish the Lord Baby Jesus done give me that eye," he added.

Two cannons at the south end of the fort both fired at the same time. Within seconds, several return volleys pummeled that section of the fort, sending a dark plume rising directly above the area from which the fort's cannons had fired.

"Them be Parrot cannons," Nat said.

Patrick nodded absently. Shots that exact had to be from one or more of the Union ships' Parrot Rifles, the rifled cannons federal ships carried to supplement their more numerous smoothbores. The Union preferred the additional firepower provided by smoothbores, willing to sacrifice accuracy to achieve it. In the Confederate Navy, where powder was at a premium, Parrot Rifles were more prevalent.

"I wish I was there," Nat said wistfully.

"You'll get your turn, Nat, you'll get your turn."

CHAPTER 10

Caleb huddled with his gun crew in the bombproof beneath Mound Battery. He felt each Union shell as it slammed into the parapets and wall above him. There would be the distant boom of the offshore cannon, dulled by the earthen walls, the faint whistle of the arcing shell, and then the thudding explosion. With each strike, particles of dust and debris fluttered out from between the timbers that braced the walls and ceiling. The bombproof filled with a thick cloud that dimmed the light from the lanterns arranged on the floor. The men were coughing, and several had covered their mouths with kerchiefs.

Caleb was exhausted. After returning from Craig's Landing with Colonel Lamb after three a.m. and seeing Daisy Lamb and the children safely across the river, he had resumed his station atop Mound Battery. There being no further activity from the anchored Union fleet, he was about to send his gun crew to their bombproofs when a sentry announced that the Union ships were moving.

He had watched in the predawn light as the battle lines approached the shore. The men around him did not speak. The usual forced bravado was absent, and Caleb could hear the waves crashing on the beach in front of the sea wall.

Lieutenant Daniel Pinson joined them. "They won't fire until we do."

"Do they think themselves gentlemen?" Private Peydreau asked.

"No," the lieutenant answered, "but they'll count our cannons as we fire and get a range."

"We always could not fire at all," Caleb mused whimsically, "and then the battle would never begin."

Lieutenant Pinson smiled.

As the rising sun lit the sea, five ironclads formed up in front of the other gunboats and slowly moved as one toward the shore, maintaining a straight line.

"They'll come the closest," the lieutenant said, indicating the ironclads, "and pound the seaface cannons. They'll try to destroy them before we can damage any ships. The gunboats will pound the landing zone and the landface. At least, that is what I would do."

The ships glided steadily in.

"Are you loaded?" Lieutenant Pinson asked. Caleb just looked at him.

"Very good," the lieutenant said briskly. "When they are close enough, they'll drop anchor. Then they're a stationary target."

"And then we blast them?" Private Peydreau asked anxiously.

Caleb could tell the youngster was trying to mask nervousness.

"We blast them," the lieutenant answered. "Then we run like hell."

"Run?" Peydreau asked incredulously. "What do you mean 'run'?" But Caleb could tell that the private was not totally opposed to the notion.

Caleb answered. "After we fire, that fleet is going to launch a hellfire the likes of which the Good Book never imagined. And it's going to be directed this way. Anyone up here will be dead within a few rounds."

The private was confused. "So, we just fire once and run away?"

"We fire at intervals," the lieutenant said.

"What do we do between them?" Peydreau asked.

"Try to stay alive," Caleb answered.

The ironclads slowed. Caleb lifted his glasses and swung them northward. The men on Pulpit Battery were already taking cover with their backs to the parapet while the gunners made final adjustments. Standing tall behind the sandbagged parapet was Colonel Lamb. Caleb marveled at the courage of the fort's commander and wondered what it must be like going to battle knowing that you had a wife who loved you and was waiting. His thoughts turned to Elizabeth, and he felt comfortable knowing she was safe in Wilmington. Probably with the Lonergens. Strange couple, the Lonergens, but Caleb liked them well enough.

"They're heaving to," Lieutenant Pinson announced.

Caleb lowered his glasses and turned his attention back to his gun.

"Steady, men," he said.

Corporal Jennings handed his sergeant the botefeux, which Caleb took with his left hand. It already held a lit match. He rechecked the gun's touch hole to ensure it was clear of debris, even though he had already checked it several times that morning. *Nerves*, he told himself. He hoped the men weren't noticing.

"There go the anchors," the lieutenant announced.

"Their gunboats are still moving," Corporal Jennings said.

"Damn," Caleb said.

"We going for the ironclads?" Peydreau asked. His voice was starting to squeak.

Caleb shook his head. "A waste of time. The gunboats in the rear have wooden hulls." But if the gunboats were still moving, he feared the battle might begin before he could get a shot at one.

"Corporal!" Caleb demanded. "Get me a line on that second on the right."

"I think it's the *Alabama*," the lieutenant said. "Then the *Montgomery*, then the *Monticello*."

"We can't go by name," Caleb sighed. "The *Montgomery* is too far behind. It's blocked from view."

"*Alabama* it is," the corporal answered. "Just don't tell my cousin about our first shot. Got it!"

"Clear away, men!" Caleb commanded, and the soldiers turned, ducked, and blocked their ears.

Just to the north, two cannons on Pulpit Battery fired simultaneously in an explosion of smoke and flame. *I guess I won't fire the first shot,* Caleb thought as he touched the botefeux to the touch hole. The thirty-two-pounder exploded with its own smoke and flame and wrenched backwards. On his own battery, two other cannons also exploded in anger.

"Git!" Lieutenant Pinson screamed, and the men rushed for the ladder. Caleb and the lieutenant waited for the three crews to start down before following. He turned and cast one last look to sea and saw the guns from the ironclad *New Ironsides* launch their own explosion from the ship's aft battery. Then he was down the ladder as the Union's return fire ripped into the parapet above him.

Once inside the bombproof, Caleb counted his crew while Lieutenant Pinson went off to report. Everyone had made it.

"What time is it?" he asked no one in particular.

"Just after eight thirty," a soldier answered.

I wonder, he thought, *how long we can last.*

Despite the heavy pounding, the hours since had passed in relative monotony. Caleb and the men stayed inside the bombproofs, their backs to the sea-facing wall and away from the open doorways to the parade ground. Shots were systematically destroying those few barracks in the parade ground that remained after the Christmas attack.

The lanterns were on the floor. No need to have the percussion from an especially powerful shell knock them off a wall or table and start a fire. No lanterns were allowed in the powder room where the fort's two walls met at a right angle.

The expressions on the surrounding faces varied. Some sat sullenly, their backs planted against the wall. One soldier twisted his hat in front of his face, as if the cloth could stop any violent shrapnel that found its way behind Fisher's earthen barriers. A sallow-faced soldier across from Caleb prayed aloud.

Next to him, a soldier grabbed Caleb's knee. "Why are they doing this?" he pleaded.

"It's war," Caleb answered simply. "The walls will hold."

"No," the soldier answered, suddenly becoming argumentative. "I don't mean the war. I mean *this,*" he said, waving his hand around. "Why won't they just leave us alone?"

Caleb was confused. "The Union Navy?"

The man shook his head. "Not the navy, the Yankees. Why don't they just leave us alone?"

"That's right," a voice across the way answered. In the thickening dust, Caleb could not identify the speaker.

"Why can't they just leave North Carolina alone?" the voice persisted. "What we do down here is our own business. What right does Washington have to say what we can and cannot do? It's none of their damn business."

"You say it!" the sallow-faced soldier agreed, momentarily halting his prayer. "It ain't no business of no federal government what we do here. We don't go up to Boston or Hartford and tell them."

"Or Jew York," another voice piped up. Another round of laughter erupted, halting quickly when a series of explosions rocked the parade ground, again kicking dust and debris through the open doorway.

"That be a good one," another voice said. "I'll have to remember that one."

"It's true," the sallow-faced soldier said. "This is our state, and we have nothing to do with them that be up in Washington. We doing just fine without them. What right do they have to tell us what we can and can't do with our own darkies?"

There was a murmur of assent. "It ain't *their* darkies," another added.

"We did just fine here without them federals," the sallow-faced soldier repeated. "Wilmington does just fine. Before the war, there was huge ships that come in here with all sorts of trade. All day long, every day. Night too, once they got that lighthouse at the mouth of the Cape Fear. Why, after they done got rid of the pirates, Wilmington become a very busy port."

There was more murmured assent.

"And there was no need for Washington to tell us what to do back then, so why now?"

Lieutenant Pinson was back. "It's time," he said.

Caleb nodded and stood up.

"And they've blasted the telegraph station to hell," Pinson added contritely.

Caleb paused and stared momentarily at his lieutenant.

"I know," the lieutenant added, raising a hand. "But it's done. We'll have to send a signalman to Battery Buchanan to flag a signal to Battery Lamb across the river to be telegraphed up."

Caleb didn't answer. The plan was to run out and return fire every thirty minutes. He gestured to his crew. Everyone stood but Private Peydreau. Lieutenant Pinson started to say something, but Caleb cut him off.

"There'll be too many if he goes. It'll give the Yankees too big a target atop the parapet."

The lieutenant turned to Caleb, opened his mouth to speak again, and then just nodded.

"Let's go," Caleb said. He dashed out of the bombproof's doorway and spun to the ladder. He took the steps two at a time and heard his crew clamber behind him.

Atop Mound Battery, the crew deftly spun a thirty-two-pounder. There was no need to swab—it had been sitting for thirty minutes. The powder was jammed in, and Caleb rammed it and a shell home, just as the crew swung the gun back. Caleb reached out and the corporal placed the lit botefeux in his left hand. Not much time to aim.

"I got one," the corporal shouted while simultaneously making the adjustments. As soon as he backed away, the rest of the crew spun to the wall without a command, and Caleb lit the touch hole. The cannon roared.

As the rest of his crew raced for the ladder, Caleb delayed just long enough to watch the shell arc over a side-wheeled federal gunboat.

Another miss. Damn.

CHAPTER 11

One mile off Federal Point, Fort Fisher
January 13, 1865

Private Jim Jeffereds stared down at the launch, bobbing on the ocean below. He wasn't afraid of boats—he was just troubled that they went on water. A private in Company H of the 27th Regiment, US Colored Troops, he never thought he'd be having anything to do with boats when he enlisted back in Ohio.

"C'mon, move it, soldiers," a white officer behind him barked.

Reluctantly, Private Jeffereds handed his Springfield musket, canteen, backpack with three days' supply of hardtack, and cartridge box with forty rounds to the sailor standing next to him and swung his leg over the side of the transport. He began descending the draped cargo netting. When he was a few feet from the launch, he reached back with his right foot, trying to find a gunwale.

"One more step, then just step back and slide down," a sailor manning an oar in the launch said kindly. "It's the easiest way."

Jim did as he was told, and when his foot touched the bottom of the boat, he made the mistake of letting go of the rope instead of reaching for the side of the launch with his hand first. He sprawled on his rear end in the boat.

"You're fine, laddie," the sailor said. "Just slide over to the far side and allow the next man in. This is the easy part. We'll do all the work."

Jim found his seat and slid over against a sailor at an oar on the far side. The sailor didn't look at him. Once settled, Jim looked around.

Thirty feet in front of him, soldiers were climbing over the side of the transport into another boat, much smaller than the one in which he sat. He was grateful to be in the larger rowboat. His was manned by twenty sailors, each at an oar. In the rear, a sailor stood at a tiller.

The cutters like the one in front of him were smaller, manned by six sailors. He wondered if the extra size and additional oarsmen of his launch meant it would be faster getting to shore.

Private William Carney slid up against him. "We be goin' now, Jimmy," he said proudly. "The whole company be getting in."

Jim studied the other transports anchored off Federal Point, five miles north of Fort Fisher. He recognized some from the harbor at Hampton Roads, where he and the other soldiers had boarded the transports seven days earlier. There was the *North Point,* the *Montauk,* even the *Russia* was there. He had tried to count them as they sailed from Hampton Roads to Beaufort, where they had stood at anchor for five days. Those days had been the hardest. No one from any unit had been allowed to get off, lest they talk about their destination.

They had languished in Beaufort Harbor—eating bad food, calling out to soldiers they knew on other ships, playing checkers, and checking and rechecking their weapons. Conditions were crowded, and men were on edge.

Yesterday morning, they had weighed anchor, and the fleet, transports, and gunboats had sailed from Beaufort, anchoring off Fort Fisher. On the way, he had variously counted nineteen, eighteen, and once seventeen transports, which he knew must be wrong.

The more important number to Jim was nine thousand—the number of soldiers aboard those army transports. Now, in every direction around him, men, white and black, were pouring over the sides of their ships and being rowed less than one mile to shore. Already a number of rowboats had landed their soldiers and were on their way back for more.

Overhead, shells screamed from the Union warships, located in a straight line farther offshore. Jim could see the projectiles and follow their trajectory as they made their way landward before screaming into the earth. They exploded in the woods and scrub beyond the section of beach where the rowboats were discharging their passengers.

With each strike, dirt and dust flew up. He studied the men, soaked to their waists, who moved quickly up the beach to form a defensive skirmish line. The soldiers weren't firing, and some of the newer arrivals just stood around on the sand, helping other soldiers come ashore through the surf, rifles and cartridge boxes held high above their heads. Occasionally, a soldier stepped into a hole or tripped and temporarily disappeared from view, only to be grabbed by others and helped ashore. From where he sat, the waves breaking on the shore did not seem that high.

When his launch was filled, several sailors climbed down the netting, making a human chain that ran from the deck to the launch. Muskets, backpacks, cartridge boxes, and canteens were passed down the human conveyor and distributed to their owners below. When the rifles and supplies were all in the boat, an officer leaned over the top rail and called, "Does every man have his weapon and supplies?"

When no one answered negatively, the officer ended his salute with a point toward the land. The human chain scrambled back up aboard ship, and the sailors in the launch pushed off and began pulling for the shore. As the launch slid away, the sailors and soldiers still aboard the transport let out cheer after cheer. On the other transports, sailors were rendering similar huzzahs.

"Don't look like them rebs want a fight on the beach," Private Carney said buoyantly, craning his neck toward the approaching sand.

"Don't worry about that," Jim said. "They'll fight someplace, just like at Petersburg."

"Well, leastways, they ain't in those woods. I guess the navy be putting too big a hit in there."

Satisfied that the rebels were not challenging the Union forces on the beach, Jim's worries turned elsewhere. As the launch in which he sat drew nearer to land, the waves crashing onshore that looked small a mile out grew before his eyes.

"You know how to swim?" Private Carney asked nervously.

Jim didn't answer. It was a cloudless day, and he estimated the air temperature to be around forty. He didn't suppose the ocean would feel much warmer.

Behind him, the Union gunboats maintained their bombardment of the scrub and pines. With each cannon boom, soldiers in the launch instinctively looked skyward to catch the flight of the shell. Jim noted that the eyes of the sailors rhythmically pulling the oars never wavered from the rear horizon.

He studied the men in the other boats as they landed, to learn which technique was most successful. Some soldiers jumped from their boats, others rolled cautiously over the side while keeping a grip on the gunwale. A few tried to step off one foot at a time. There was no consistency as to the best method.

Thirty yards from shore, the launch grated on the soft sand and tilted to one side.

"Alright boys," the sailor standing at the tiller called out. "Jump for it."

The sailor next to him moved aside, and Jim lifted his gear and stood up. Balancing as best he could, he moved to the edge of the launch. He stared at the surf swirling around the beached craft, trying to judge the depth.

"Jump with both feet, men," the kind sailor offered from the other side. "If you do one foot at a time, you'll pitch forward like a drunk on a Saturday night."

The sailors roared. Not wanting to show cowardice, Jim jumped with both feet, his rifle held aloft. He sank in over his head and realized, even as salt water rushed into his mouth and up his nose, that he had landed in a hole. He started to choke and tip forward, still trying to hold his rifle aloft. He felt that he was about to fall face forward when he felt a pair of strong arms pull him upright and his head out of the water.

"You're fine, boy."

It was the sailor he had sat next to in the launch, who hadn't looked at him or said a word all the way in. The sailor had jumped in and, like Jim, was now standing chest deep in freezing seawater.

"Just breathe, soldier," the sailor added. "Cough it out."

Jim complied as the sailor held him. Other men toppled out of the boat with varying degrees of success. There were at least four sailors in the water assisting them.

When the last soldier was off the launch, the kind sailor yelled, "Hey, lads, give us a shove out, will ya?"

The last two soldiers handed off their rifles and then turned and pushed the launch back until it slid off the sand and leveled. Working as one against the pounding surf, the sailors turned the launch smoothly around and started back toward the waiting transports.

Jim waded ashore. The soldiers already on the beach whooped and hollered as each boat came in and soldiers got dunked. A white officer in an obviously brand-new uniform, who was standing at the bow of a boat, tried to step off in a dignified manner, only to get dunked face first. Those on the beach let out an especially loud howl.

Several men started small campfires and attempted to dry out socks, pants, and other clothing. A few checked their rifles and paper cartridges.

Jim spotted the signal flag for the 27th Colored Regiment and headed up the beach toward where it stood, firmly planted in the sand.

Captain Pinney, in command of Company H, welcomed each man as he approached. All the officers of the 27th, as in all colored regiments formed after the War Department's order in May 1863, were white. The highest rank a colored man could reach was sergeant.

"Settle down," the captain said. "Try to dry out. We'll set up here and await orders. Until then, try to rest. We've a skirmish line at the edge of the woods, but no sign of the enemy."

Jim dropped to one knee on the sand and checked his rifle. They had been fortunate today. After the Christmas attack, the rebels had abandoned the two batteries that had guarded this part of Federal Point at the tip of Myrtle Sound. If the rebels had kept them manned, those batteries could have raised havoc with the boats coming ashore. Even better, no one had fought them on the beach.

William Carney flopped down next to Jim and stripped off his shoes, socks, and pants. Several of the other men from Company H started their own fires, and soldiers soon crowded around, trying to place their clothing as near as possible.

A sergeant ran up to the captain and excitedly announced that he had spotted a herd of cattle just on the other side of the scrub.

"What are you waiting for, then?" Captain Pinney bellowed. "It's meat or hardtack. You choose."

A sergeant from another company of the 27th setting up nearby selected a few men, and off they went to scavenge meat for dinner.

No, Private Jeffereds thought, *this may go a lot better than I feared.*

CHAPTER 12

Colonel Newton Martin Curtis, commander of the First Brigade, Second Division, of the Union's XXIV Army Corps, stood atop a pile of food crates and directed his brigade's ammunition and other supplies to storage. It was really a major's job, but Colonel Curtis—the former lawyer, schoolteacher, and farmer—was a stickler who liked to oversee even the smallest details.

Besides, standing and directing was fairly mindless, and it gave him a chance to reflect. On this day, he reflected on the number of items for which he could give thanks. He was grateful it wasn't raining. He was grateful that the weather, though crisp, was not freezing. He was grateful that not one man had been lost coming ashore. He was grateful that the landing was unchallenged.

And finally, he decided, he was grateful to be back on Federal Point, to have been granted a second chance. In December, he had waded ashore on Christmas Day, just as he had today, before slinking back aboard ship two days later, frustrated and furious with the command decision to leave. Now, just three weeks later, he was back, without the commander who had ordered the earlier retreat.

Fort Fisher lay five miles south. His six-foot-five-inch height atop the crates gave him a good vantage point from which to direct cargo traffic, but he still couldn't see the fort through the pines. He could, however, hear the naval bombardment as shell after shell pounded it. Occasionally, he paused to stare southward, following a particularly devastating combination of explosions. But he knew better than to think that naval action alone would be sufficient.

A captain from his regiment approached hesitantly.

"Sir, there's a civilian asking to speak with you."

Colonel Curtis swore to himself without pausing in his work. It was those damn cattle. The troops had located a wandering herd, and steaks were sizzling all around.

"Tell him they are Confederate spoils of war, subject to seizure. He'll need to make a claim for his livestock with the Claims Office at the War Department."

He sensed the captain's hesitation.

"It's not the cattle, sir."

"Then what the devil?"

"It's a woman, sir. Says she knows you."

"Where?"

His glare flew behind the captain. There, fifty yards away, she stood. He stopped directing and stared. She held her horse's reins in her right hand. A sergeant next to her appeared to have her under guard. She was wearing men's pants and a long coat that was overlarge for her. She was bare headed, and her hair was pulled back and tied behind her head. Her dirty face was streaked with sweat. The horse was soaked and panting. She had been riding hard and, he gathered from the horse's condition, for a long time.

"Damn!" he muttered. "Goddamn."

"Shall I send her away, sir?"

"Only if you're a damn fool, Captain," he said softly without taking his eyes off her. He climbed down from the crates, jumping the last step to the ground. He tugged off his gloves and gestured to the sergeant, who saluted before retreating.

He strode toward her. She was shivering, and he guessed she had been on the horse all night. The captain walked along with his superior officer, looking back and forth between his colonel and the woman. After studying the colonel's facial expression, he also withdrew wordlessly.

"Missus Tuckerman," the colonel said when he came up to her. "What a lovely animal."

He wasn't sure if he should shake her hand, bow, or hug her.

She smiled, apparently sensing his discomfort.

"Why, Colonel, you never wrote."

He laughed. "I see you maintain your charming sense of humor."

"Thank you, but I do mean it. I thought someone would have contacted the league again."

Soldiers scurried past with materiel. Colonel Curtis called to a major and instructed him where to place the regiment's supplies. When a private carrying a large bundle in front of his face bumped him, Curtis pulled Elizabeth aside.

"Come, walk with me," he said and led her and the horse to a quieter, open space in the scrub.

"Why should I have been in contact? Do you have more news? I was told about your reports at Hampton Roads. You are lucky you didn't ride into a pitched battle. I expected the rebels to be waiting for us when we came ashore."

"We took care of Hoke," she said.

Colonel Curtis paused in his walk and turned to stare at the woman with whom he and Colonel Comstock had once spent a cold Christmas night in a rifle pit, just one hundred fifty yards from the entrance to Fort Fisher. Her statement shocked him on two accounts.

"Hoke?" he asked dumbly. "Our intelligence service says Hoke has been sent south, to challenge Sherman."

She raised one eyebrow in that way that annoyed him.

"Intelligence service?" she asked. "Really? Would that be the intelligence service sitting behind their desks in Washington or the ones sitting behind their desks in Hampton Roads?"

She was exasperating. "Madam—" he began.

She pointed north and interrupted him. "Hoke's division got pulled off the peninsula in December after you all left. Bragg has kept him in Wilmington for parades ever since, and my information suggests he's equipping Hoke for an attack on New Bern."

"Are you sure?" he asked.

"Well, if you had read the later dispatches from the league, the ones I sent to Beaufort, you would know this. And yes, I am sure. I'm about an hour's hard ride ahead of his whole division. And in case you care to know, a detachment of the Second South Carolina Cavalry has been detailed to keep tabs on you."

"The second?"

"They crossed in front of me on the Wilmington Road. I exchanged pleasantries with them. One of them asked if his shirt was ready," she added dourly, "and advised me to seek shelter as there were Yankees about."

"Damn!" He knew much, much better than to doubt her. "And, pray tell," he asked, "how did you divert General Hoke?"

She shrugged. "It was not too difficult, although it certainly would have been easier if I had been told when you were coming, instead of hearing about it from someone who reads Northern newspapers."

"And?" he pressed. He turned, and the pair resumed their walk, the horse clopping along with them. *We must look like a rich married couple,* he thought. *A husband out walking with his equestrian wife.*

"I watched the fleet arrive last night," Elizabeth said. "It was not the greatest military strategy. Arriving at night and anchoring in plain sight of the fort, allowing time for a telegraphed message to Bragg. You should have planned the arrival for morning and landed immediately. You're lucky Hoke wasn't here to greet you. Another West Point decision?"

He shook his head. This woman was so forthright, so . . . so . . . confident. That was it! Confident. He had never met a woman like this. He wondered who else had—and if they had managed better than he.

In front of them, the 27th Regiment was marching forward to dig in. The world was changing around him. Colored soldiers, a woman talking like a man. Hell, thinking like a man.

He ignored the West Point comment. They had had this discussion before, in the rifle pit Christmas night. Hell, he had said similar things. He wasn't a West Pointer either, and she knew it.

"So, how did you interfere?" he asked again.

"Partly luck. I rode hard to Wilmington. The fort had telegraphed a message to General Bragg, and a coast watcher had also spotted the fleet. One of the league members was on duty at the telegraph office and delayed them."

"How?" he asked. "They would hang him for a spy if they caught him."

Elizabeth laughed. "This is the South, Colonel. They don't hang drinking men. I got him a bottle, and he got himself drunk. Blamed it on the whiskey. Oh, I'm sure they cursed him like hell, but Bragg didn't get the message until the middle of the night, and by the time he got Hoke on the move, it was too late to do anything here. But he's coming." She looked back up the peninsula.

Colonel Curtis winced. It was one thing for women to think like men, another for them to use profanity. And referring to General Bragg and General Hoke as Bragg and Hoke, enemies or not, why, he might do that among his own peers, but, well . . . well, was she a peer? He quickly shrugged off the thought.

"So, they are on their way."

She nodded. "They'll set up a skirmish line below Sugar Loaf so they can land supplies. I'd say just beyond those woods." She pointed.

He did not discount what she said. The memory of that Christmas night flooded back to him. His New Yorkers had been within two hundred yards of Shepherd's Battery, guarding the west end of Fort Fisher's landface. He was ready. His men were ready. Behind him, more troops poured ashore, prepared to support his attack. The navy had bombarded the fort all day on the twenty-fourth and twenty-fifth and driven the defenders off the wall. His men had landed on the twenty-fifth. It had seemed so open, so vulnerable. He could sense victory. One charge and his men could take that fort. He knew it, he absolutely knew it.

"Give me fifty men, and I can take it," he had said to Comstock and Elizabeth.

"Do it," Comstock had said.

"Don't be that foolish," Elizabeth had warned.

"Then give me my brigade, and I'll take it," he countered.

But General Butler, who had taken control of the expedition, announced that conditions were not ripe and ordered a retreat. He sent a messenger to Curtis.

It was General Weitzel, the expedition's original commander, who had introduced Newton Curtis to Elizabeth Tuckerman, the local Loyal Union League president and chief federal spy in the area. And it was to General Weitzel that Colonel Curtis had intended to turn, desperate for someone to intercede with General Butler.

And this damn woman had been so helpful. She had led Colonels Comstock and Curtis forward to a depression she knew within yards of the fort. There the three had lain in the dark while Missus Tuckerman had reviewed each and every battery located along the landface—reciting the firepower of each, the number of rounds available for each, and the number, condition, and training of the men who defended each section of the wall.

Lying in the dirt next to her, Newton Curtis had listened, transfixed. It was not just her knowledge and commitment, it was—he admitted reluctantly—that she was a woman.

"And now?" he asked.

"There's maybe eight hundred fifty soldiers inside. They hope to reinforce the garrison with whatever men Hoke can spare. They will come down by steamer. Getting some firepower on the river will help, if any of your men can hit a moving steamer," she added with a smirk. "Even if they can't, the steamer will be manned by civilian river sailors, and being shot at might be enough to turn them around."

Colonel Curtis nodded. "The fleet," he said simply. "The fleet can drop shells in the river, but they'll have no line of sight to their target."

"That may not matter," she said. "It might be enough to drive them to the far bank or even back up to Wilmington."

She stared across the peninsula toward the river, as if seeing the battle unfold.

If women could ever go to West Point, he mused, they would be crazy not to take her. He laughed at the thought. Women in the military, indeed.

Behind him, members of the 27th began to sing as they continued digging.

"Munitions?" he asked.

"Maybe three thousand rounds. No exact count. They've done some live firing for new soldiers this past week, and there's been no resupply. They aren't expecting you till spring."

He nodded absently. She had been convincing with Colonel Comstock Christmas night. Either that or she had successfully shamed him. They had dispatched a runner in an effort to change General Butler's mind. After the runner had left, Curtis had stayed in the rifle pit with her—studying the fort, looking at the stars, and talking. They were confident that a messenger would return with positive news.

They had discussed everything in topics ranging from their pasts, to his wife, to Elizabeth's late husband, and even to her relationship with the Confederate sergeant now hunkered down five miles to the south. Through all the talking, he had not wanted to leave her side to return to his men, though he knew he should.

He cleared his throat. "Missus Tuckerman," he began hesitantly, "are you still friends with that young man from Wilmington?"

She didn't answer or look at him, but continued staring straight across the peninsula.

"It must be difficult," he continued awkwardly. "All that you do, knowing what the effect might be. On him."

She spun and looked full at the colonel. Her eyes blazed.

"Having someone to love, and being loved in return, is God's greatest gift to humankind," she said. "But God has allowed scourges to be placed on this earth and charged us with ridding them. There are times, Colonel, when the lives of two people mean less than the pile of sand beneath our feet.

"This is a great scourge, Colonel, and it will only be washed by the blood of brother against brother, neighbor against neighbor. When it is over, and only then, can we again accept God's greatest gift."

She turned and rubbed her horse between its ears. The mare nuzzled her.

She smiled again, adopting the twisted facial expression he had come to know as they lay in the pit and watched the stars on Christmas night.

"And you, Colonel," she said, now running her hand back along her horse's withers, "above all, should know what this war has done and how it affects those we love. As you told me three weeks ago, you are married to the former Phoebe Davis, are you not? A cousin to Jefferson Davis. You fight the war, and yet you still love, as I'm sure Missus Curtis does also her cousin."

"Well, yes," he stammered, "I see what you mean."

"Do you?" she asked sharply, turning back to him. "Your marriage to Phoebe invites snickers and snide comments from your fellow officers, yet it deters you not from your duty."

The colonel nodded. This woman, this Elizabeth Tuckerman, was a whole different story from anyone he had ever met. He found it hard to accept that, at twenty-nine years old, he was actually one year her senior.

He had been the last soldier to leave on December twenty-seventh, wading to the waiting launch from the USS Nereus. As the sailors rowed him away, he had turned back and watched Missus Tuckerman, standing alone on the rise above the beach. Neither had waved.

"Madam," he finally said, looking her straight in the eyes. "Please do not think me brash when I say that I think you will again marry. And when you do, I do not know whether I will feel eternally sorry for the poor wretch or spend the rest of my mortal days envying him."

CHAPTER 13

Fort Fisher

January 13, 1865

Caleb and Lieutenant Pinson turned left out of the bombproof's doorway and monkey-walked along the inner side of the fort's seaface. When they reached the open terrain at the end of the earthen wall, they broke into a trot, Caleb quickly gaining the lead. He could hear Lieutenant Pinson huffing along behind him.

Maybe that is why I feel so compelled to run by myself, Caleb mused, *to get my body and lungs prepared for moments like this.* Moments when Union naval artillery would target him as he crossed open fields. He slowed momentarily, allowing the lieutenant to catch up. He then sprinted off at a faster pace.

He couldn't remember exactly when he'd developed his love of running. He wasn't especially fast, and hadn't won many races as a boy, but he had run quite a bit during his half year at Bowdoin, often rising before dawn. Perhaps his running at college had been motivated by a desire to evade the uncomfortable conversations he could never seem to avoid as war loomed.

He had taken the opportunity to slip from rooms when he sensed the conversation was heading that way, but as the election of 1860 inched closer, escape had become more difficult. And for some reason, the conversation always seemed to turn at him, rather than include him.

"Look," he once tried to explain, "slavery has nothing to do with it."

When the indignant shouts and guffaws had died down, Caleb tried again. "It is a matter of everyone being allowed to decide for themselves what to do."

He waited for the new round of catcalls to subside before continuing.

"Supposing North Carolina decides that they no longer want to allow slavery?" he argued, turning toward a student who was particularly aggressive. "Shouldn't we be allowed to abolish it, just like Massachusetts and New Hampshire and other states have?"

When he received the expected assents, he continued.

"Why, what if the federal government then said that we couldn't? That doing so constitutes the taking of property in violation of the Constitution as it affects property interests in other states that do commerce through North Carolina? Would you all say that the federal government in Washington should be allowed to dictate to North Carolina that they can't abolish slavery?"

When the chorus of "no's" died away, Caleb pressed on.

"Well then, if the federal government can't tell North Carolina that they can't abolish slavery, that it's a states' rights issue, how can they tell North Carolina that they *must* abolish it? Whether it is the federal government or a state that is for or against slavery is just the luck of the dice roll. The question is whether what North Carolina does can be dictated by Washington. Slavery is a false issue in all this."

The room erupted, as it always did at this point, drowning out any further efforts by Caleb to explain state autonomy under the United States Constitution.

To Caleb, it answered the question posed the day before by Elizabeth, the one to which he had been unable to respond. The issue was one of self-determination. Each state should be allowed to make decisions for itself, right or wrong, without interference from others. What North Carolina did should remain up to North Carolina. And soldiers from Massachusetts or New Hampshire or Maine had no right to come down to his state and dictate what North Carolina should do.

He also didn't think it right for soldiers from North Carolina to march up to Pennsylvania, like they had two years earlier, to fight in that

Gettysburg field. It was why he was a sergeant in the 36th North Carolina Artillery and not an officer fighting farther north.

He never said any of this to Elizabeth. As with his fellow students at Bowdoin, she would never understand. To Elizabeth, as to his fellow students, it was all about the end. They believed slavery was evil and should be eradicated. However that was accomplished did not matter. Self-determination did not matter, the Constitution did not matter, and the rule of law did not matter. The goal had to be achieved at any cost.

"What will this federation be worth if you destroy every institution, break every law, to abolish slavery?" he would shout to a room full of students now out of control.

He had tried a different tack. "We all agree that criminals should not roam free on our streets, do we not? But, to make our society safer, should we enlist the army to go house to house, smashing doors to uncover evidence of crime? Certainly, afterwards, our society would be safer, but at what cost?"

"But slavery is wrong!" they would bellow, and the verbal assault upon him would resume.

Now on the field of battle to defend his beliefs, Caleb crouched behind a solitary tree and waited for the lieutenant to catch up again. When he did, he slumped next to the sergeant, panting. It was about a mile from the fort to Battery Buchanan, where Lieutenant Pinson had seen a steamer heading earlier. He had asked Caleb to accompany him to the landing behind the battery to discover what was afoot.

Although it had not been an order, Caleb had readily agreed. It might be supplies or munitions sent down from Wilmington or, even better, men to reinforce the paltry eight hundred fifty soldiers still garrisoned. With the fort's telegraph office in splinters, communication with Wilmington had been reduced to sending runners to Battery Buchanan. They would signal across the river to Battery Lamb, which still had a working telegraph office. The pair had no idea why the steamer was approaching.

Caleb looked back at the earthen fort. The destruction seen by New Orleans, Vicksburg, and Georgia had finally come to the Cape Fear River. The barrage was so heavy that Colonel Lamb had cut back on return fire. Even every thirty minutes was too risky. The return fire was designed to keep the Union fleet at bay and off the landface, but it was not working. The federal bombardment was constant—much heavier and more accurate than in December. Already, most of the seaface guns were knocked out. The balance of the fleet's firepower was now being directed at the landface cannons. Caleb knew that many of those had already been knocked off their carriages or otherwise damaged. If the fort were not reinforced, the coming land battle would not end well.

"Ready?" Caleb asked.

The lieutenant only nodded while continuing to gasp. Caleb gave him another minute to catch his breath. It was not that long a run, but sprinting across an open field while fearing the Union Navy was targeting you did little for relaxation. Still, he doubted whether the gunboats would target two individual soldiers running away from the fort.

"Let's go," Caleb announced and stood and resumed his sprint. When they got within one hundred yards of Battery Buchanan, Caleb increased his speed to a full-out dash.

The pair circled around to the opening and entered yet another dimly lit bombproof. Inside, a soldier in a general's uniform stood flanked by two staff officers speaking with a gun crew.

In the flickering light, Caleb didn't recognize the general. A panting Lieutenant Pinson pushed past and saluted.

"General Whiting!" the lieutenant said.

Whereas Braxton Bragg was overall commander of the area, General Chase Whiting was in charge of the Cape Fear Defense System. It included Fort Fisher, under the command of Colonel Lamb.

Caleb glanced around the small shelter beneath the battery. There were no supplies and no additional men.

General Whiting explained that he and his two staff officers, who he introduced as Major Hill and Lieutenant Fairly, had just disembarked and wanted to be brought to Colonel Lamb. The steamer's only cargo had been the three passengers.

"Will you be taking control of the fort, General?" Lieutenant Pinson asked. As the highest-ranking officer now at Fort Fisher, it was his right.

The general reiterated that he was only there to consult with Colonel Lamb and offer assistance.

"Bring them to Colonel Lamb," Pinson said, turning to Caleb. "I will be along shortly."

Caleb led the trio out of the battery and back the way he had come. To his surprise, the three officers almost kept up with him, and he only slowed his speed twice. If the Union Navy spotted the four, it didn't target them.

Back at Fort Fisher, Caleb led them through the first open doorway and along the tunnel that wound through the interconnecting rooms beneath the seaface. Under the Northeast Bastion, he found Colonel Lamb engrossed with his assistants.

"General!" Colonel Lamb exclaimed when he turned around.

"I have come to see how my creation is holding up and to share your fate."

The colonel's expression hardened, and he lowered his voice.

"Not well, I fear. The Yankees are giving us more of a pounding than last month. I can't send my men out to return even token fire, not that it would do any good. They've driven us off the parapets and hit our seaface pretty good. They are degrading the landface. Their army stands not more than five miles north. They'll attack tomorrow or the next day. I fear that we will be forced to try to stop seven or eight thousand. Our cannons will be gone by then. It is grim, indeed, without help, sir. We need General Bragg to attack now."

"How many men do we have?" General Whiting asked.

"Eight hundred able-bodied, possibly less. With General Bragg coming south, we can still trap the Yankees on the beach where they camp."

"Don't count on him, Colonel," General Whiting said. "When I left Wilmington, he was drawing up a new defensive line to save Wilmington when the fort falls. He is already evacuating equipment and supplies in anticipation of our surrender."

Colonel Lamb stared at his new arrival speechlessly before slumping back against the wall. "I will yield command to you, sir."

The general shook his head vigorously. "No need for that. But we will be on our own."

"If only General Bragg had attacked when the Yankees came ashore," Colonel Lamb said. "We telegraphed Wilmington upon spotting the fleet."

"As did a coast watcher," General Whiting replied. "The telegraph operator was drunk. General Hoke didn't move until this morning and is only now getting into position. I question whether it would have mattered. General Bragg appears to have adopted a fatalistic approach.

"But there is still hope," General Whiting continued, brightening slightly. "I can bring infantry from across the river to strengthen our landface. The peninsula is narrow, with a marsh in the middle. The Yankees will have to attack in two lines. I doubt they know Hoke is here. We may have lost the cannons, Colonel, but we'll have the walls and the traverses. If God is willing, we may still prevail."

CHAPTER 14

Confederate Point, south of Wilmington
January 13, 1865

Private Seth Colburn, of the North Carolina 66th Infantry, was glad it was winter. Even with insufficient clothing, it was easier to march when it was cool. And marching he had been, for several hours.

Named after its commander, Robert Hoke, the 66th had been rousted out of its slumber early that morning. Veterans of the Petersburg fighting, they had remained in the Cape Fear area since arriving in December to stop the Yankee attack on Fort Fisher. The Yankees had fled after two days, and the division had been withdrawn to Wilmington.

There had been parties, parades, and reequipment for three weeks while rumors flew about their next destination. Some claimed they were going south to stop Sherman, others were certain they were going back to Petersburg, while a few were steadfast in their whispered assertions that General Bragg was planning an attack against New Bern. No one thought they would be needed to stop the Yankees at Fort Fisher. Not until spring.

But all that changed with the morning's bugle blare. As Seth had risen from his bedroll, shaking the ground's cold from his bones, he knew that this was not a planned operation. Officers ran to and fro, and sergeants appeared to be searching for guidance. He was told to bring all gear— later, only his musket and ammunition. He and his tent mate, Asa King, looked at each other and shook their heads.

They quickly formed up at a speed that surprised Seth, given the morning's confused start. But this was an experienced brigade of an experienced division. If anyone could do whatever they were going to be asked to, Seth was confident that Hoke's division was the right choice.

Civilians came out of their homes to watch. The early bugle call, coupled with the hurried bustle, gave rise to the civilians' suspicion that something big was afoot. Two children whooped and hollered their support, and Seth waved appreciatively in return. A farmer driving his wagon past the encampment pulled over and solemnly stood and saluted the soldiers readying to go off to do their duty. A woman on horseback, wearing what looked to be her husband's clothes and standing next to a sullen darkie, gave an appreciative smile and watched them form up before riding off.

Of course the civilians were interested. Word had spread that the Yankees were back. Seth did not believe it. However, if true, the civilians had every right to be concerned. If Fort Fisher fell, Wilmington would fall into Yankee hands, and the locals were well aware of what was happening in Georgia as Sherman drove through the state.

As Seth's unit marched, six abreast, rumors flew up and down the ranks. When they heard the distant roar of heavy cannons, the rumors flew faster. With each fusillade, the rumors became more outrageous.

"Sherman has landed at Confederate Point," a fat soldier they called Grandpa announced. "Came up from Georgia last night, he did."

"That's crap," a soldier in the rear countered.

"No, it's true," another said. "He's captured the fort and is dug in there with eighteen thousand Yankees and a fleet of three hundred warships."

"The Yankees don't have three hundred warships."

"Yes, they do, they've been building them in secret. My wife's cousin lives in Portsmouth, New Hampshire, and she watched them being built."

"You're not married."

And on it went. Next to him, Asa King said little. A third friend of theirs, Robert Dearborn, marched in the row behind.

"I don't like this," Dearborn said.

"You never like it," Asa said.

"Did you bring any food?" Seth asked.

"Naw, we'll be back tonight," Dearborn answered.

The unit halted six miles from Fort Fisher. A lieutenant ordered them to move off to the left and rest. The unit behind Seth's doubled-timed toward the river. Seth watched until it disappeared. He sat on the ground with Asa King and Robert Dearborn, rubbing his feet with his shoes off.

The lieutenant approached.

"On your feet," he commanded. "We're to form an advance skirmish line and approach the ocean. The Yankees have landed, and the cannon is their fleet's. We are to find them and report back. Then we attack in force."

"Is it Sherman?" Robert Dearborn asked.

Instead of answering, the lieutenant moved off to speak with another group of men huddling in the brisk air.

"That was a stupid question," Asa said.

"Was not," Robert responded. He appeared hurt by the rebuke.

When he saw other soldiers standing up, Seth hurriedly put his shoes back on and joined the rest of the company. Instead of marching, they spread out in a thin line and advanced southeast toward the ocean. Their conversations became whispered. The cannon booms grew louder. Seth knew they were heading the right way.

They picked their way through the pines and low brush for approximately a mile and a half. Just short of a slight rise, a sergeant raced toward them from the front and silently motioned everyone to get down. Seth dropped to his stomach, his loaded musket held in front of him. After conferring with the sergeant, the lieutenant motioned the line to stay down and move forward. Seth began crawling, keeping his head down. The line slithered slowly up the rise. On the far side, there was a break in the brush, and Seth could see through the pines several hundred yards to the ocean.

Except, he could see no beach. Blue-jacketed Yankees blanketed the area where bare sand and dunes should have been. Some stood around, some cooked food over open fires. Many were idly watching as dozens of rowboats plied back and forth between the anchored fleet and the shore. Others unloaded crates of supplies.

"Damn," Asa whispered. He looked around. "Where's the lieutenant gone?"

Robert looked back. "Looks like he didn't come up with us."

Asa swore and turned to Robert. "Go back and find an officer. Tell him the Yankees are on the sand. We have them trapped."

Dearborn was back in a few minutes with a captain. Asa and Seth pointed out the Yankees and suggested an immediate attack.

The captain said nothing, but he studied the beach area through the trees.

Seth saw movement to the left, opposite the southern edge of Myrtle Sound. A number of blue jackets moved in the brush. He shook Robert's shoulder and pointed. Asa was already aiming his rifle. Before he fired, the Yankees let loose their own volley, the white smoke rising in a line behind the brush. Confederates around him fired back, but the length of the line of white smoke told him that they were heavily outnumbered.

From his right there was more movement, and Seth spotted a regimental flag held aloft.

"It's Abbott's brigade!" he hissed, recognizing the colors he had seen outside of Petersburg.

As men around him struggled to reload, the Yankee line to his right advanced. Without waiting for orders, the Confederate skirmish line rose as one and fell back, scampering through the brush that cut at their legs. Another volley rang out behind him, and Seth heard the cries and unmistakable sounds of men falling. He did not look back.

Fifty yards to the rear was another depression, surrounded by what appeared to be old earthworks. The remnants of the Confederate skirmish line dove behind it. Men frantically attempted to finish reloading while staring back into the woods. Seth heard the crash of approaching soldiers.

The lieutenant reappeared and dispatched a soldier to the rear with instructions to bring up reinforcements.

"How many?" Robert asked in a hoarse whisper as he crouched in the hollow next to Asa.

"Can't be many," Seth answered with more confidence than he felt. "Maybe pickets."

Seth's mind flew to the line of smoke from the first Union volley. That was more than pickets. And Abbott's brigade had appeared on the right, with colors.

"Maybe a skirmish line," Seth said, amending his answer.

Next to him, Asa snorted. "Horseshit," he said.

Above and to his left, he heard the whine of artillery shells, followed by heavy booming crashes in the forest. Trees behind him toppled. *The federal fleet. Damn.*

"Here they come!" a soldier yelled.

To his right, the brush disappeared as Yankees crashed out of the woods toward them. Abbott's colors and an American flag flapped in the middle.

"They're charging," was all Seth had time to say before the captain turned and ran.

Seth hesitated for only a second. Other soldiers threw down their weapons and fled. Seth stood, caught a quick glance at Asa, drawing yet another bead, and turned and ran for the rear. He tried to stay behind the trees, constantly moving sideways to get large trunks between himself and the Yankees behind him. He did not look back, but he sensed that the Yankees were neither firing at the fleeing Confederates nor pursuing.

After a half mile he stopped, panting. Many of his fellow soldiers were empty-handed. He was surprised to discover that he still held his rifle. He looked back. The Yankees weren't coming.

When he turned, he came face to face with a major.

"What's happening, Private?" the major demanded.

Seth pointed back to the ocean and, between labored breaths, tried to explain. "They were waiting for us, sir. They were dug in. Entrenched. I ain't talking about no skirmish line. Two regiments. From Abbott's brigade. They knew we was coming."

The major looked back to where Seth was pointing. There was no sign of Yankees.

CHAPTER 15

Federal Point, North Carolina
27th United States Colored Troops
January 13-14, 1865

At nine o'clock, the sergeants had gathered everyone from their evening campfires and told them to be prepared to move with their gear. A few soldiers had opened bedrolls, hoping to get a few hours' sleep, but officers returned and lined everyone up in formation. Just before midnight, the army finally began its move.

The 27th United States Colored Troops took the lead ahead of Adelbert Ames's brigade as the Union Army marched south along the ocean toward Fort Fisher.

"Ain't it great, Jim," Private William Carney said, catching up next to him. "Us being in the lead and all."

Jim Jeffereds didn't want to turn to look at his friend. It was just two days past a full moon. The dim moonlight cast shadows, obscuring the footing, and around him, soldiers stumbled forward.

"They need someone to clear the brush," he said. "That's why they put us first."

"They're going to have us attack the fort," William argued. "Why, Abbott's men, they got left behind to keep Hoke off our backside."

"Hoke?" Jim asked, unable to resist turning. "You sure?"

"Sure enough. The sergeant have me diggin' latrines, and when I git back, all the meat was gone. None left for old William. But some of them New Hampshire white boys with Abbott call me over and give me some of theirs." William chuckled. "Them white boys sure enough slow eaters."

"You check that meat real good?" a deep voice from two rows behind asked. The soldiers laughed.

Private Carney turned and began walking backwards in the dark. "Hey, those white boys be kind to William. Anyway, they say that was Hoke's men that was skirmishing up the beach. They say that they knowed that Hoke was a-coming. They have two regiments waiting for the skirmishers. They say them rebs hightailed it back to Wilmington so fast they couldn't catch 'em."

"How they know it was Hoke?" another voice asked.

"Oh, they knowed, alright. They caught some rebs, and they said so themself."

"Sheet," a voice in front said. "Lordy damn. Those kind white boys better not be so kind in a fight, iffin' that really be Hoke on our arse."

There was more laughter all around.

"Oh, they be good fighters. Them's Abbott's men," William Carney said. "They's keep 'em offen' us, and us coloreds will take the fort."

"Well, they better do a better job than they did against Hoke up at Petersburg," a fifth soldier chimed in.

The surrounding laughter turned to solemn vocal agreement.

The column picked its way down the coast. To Jim's left, the waves crashed on the shore, and he saw the signal lamps of the anchored fleet. The gunboats had moved out of range and slackened their fire for the night. A few selected gunboats or ironclads threw occasional shots at the fort in the darkness.

"I don't reckon those rebs be gettin' much sleep," William said.

"Us neither," the deep-voiced soldier replied.

When the pine trees faded to a more open plain, the column swung west across the peninsula. Marshy thickets picked at their trousers and scratched their legs. As they neared the river, the ground rose and became drier, but the thickets worsened. The lead skirmishers were reduced to walking single file. Still in the lead, the 27th made its way to the river's edge.

Jim was ready to settle down, but pickets had located better ground nearer the fort, and the column picked up and swung south again, coming to within two miles of the landface. Officers called a halt and told the men to rest while they could.

Jim huddled in a circle with his fellows, while sergeants moved among the troops, telling everyone not to start fires.

"That's what them white Abbott boys said too," William said. "They's suppose to start a whole bunch of campfires along the beach and make them fort rebs think that we haven't moved none."

The dark outline of Fort Fisher loomed in the dim moonlight. There wasn't a fire or torch to be seen from the hulk. Occasionally, the light from an exploding shell lit up the landface. Jim wondered what it was like to have been inside during the bombardment, but he had no sympathy.

"Anyone know what day today is?" a soldier asked.

"Saturday, by now. January fourteenth," Jim answered.

William gave out a low whistle. "Tomorrow be one year."

The thought startled Jim. He hadn't thought about it, but January fifteenth marked one year since the formation of the 27th United States Colored Troops, mustered in back in Ohio.

He and William had been there from the beginning. William had been born free in Cleveland, but the two had quickly become fast friends, despite their different backgrounds.

Jim had been a slave on a sugar plantation in Mississippi. War had come, as did eventual word of the emancipation. The decree did not impact him. In the early summer of 1863, the grapevine reported the decision by the Union War Department to enlist colored troops. When Vicksburg fell in July, he saw his avenue of opportunity. He would fight for the Union and to end slavery. For Jim, it was an easy decision, but Sally, his wife, opposed him leaving. She was not afraid of retribution, but of him getting killed.

"Let them come here," she pleaded.

But Jim's mind was made up. "If I don't go, I'll always know that I didn't," he told her.

One night, while Sally slept, he whispered his good-bye and struck out for Vicksburg. He dared not stop, for he knew the slave catchers wouldn't. He made Vicksburg in two days of nonstop running and hiding, telling the Union pickets he was there to enlist.

An officer from a Union gunboat anchored in the river prodded him to enlist in the navy.

"You can join us right here, boy, on this boat, and you can fight right away," a white officer told him. "No need to walk when you can ride, and you won't have to leave Mississippi. Besides," the officer added, "the army's just enlisting coloreds now. In the navy, we've been serving with you coloreds for years already. Go ahead, talk to any of the others aboard. Many are escaped slaves, like yourself."

It was tempting. But ultimately, he didn't want to be on a boat. They went on water. With the Mississippi River in Union hands, Jim made his way along the waterway, passed along from one safe household to another. He arrived in Ohio in January, just in time to learn of the establishment of the 27th.

They had mustered the coloreds in to Camp Delaware, the Union Army camp on the banks of Ohio's Olentangy River. The camp had opened in 1862 on the west side of the river for white soldiers, specifically the 96th and 121st Ohio regiments. In 1863, a second, segregated camp opened on the east bank to train the 27th. Both were called Camp Delaware.

Arriving in Ohio just in time, Jim had enlisted and reported on the first day he was eligible to do so—January fifteenth, 1864. In May, the regiment had shipped south, originally attached to the 1st Brigade, 4th Division, 9th Corps, Army of the Potomac. Two months of guarding supply trains left Jim with the sick feeling that he would never see any real action against his oppressors.

All that had changed in July when the 27th was thrown into the Siege at Petersburg. For six months, the Union slugged it out with Confederates around Petersburg, Virginia, considered a gateway to Richmond. They had taken a beating, and their ranks were now so depleted that some of the companies had combined.

In December, with the siege languishing, the regiment had shipped aboard transports for the first attack on Fort Fisher. Now, three weeks later, they were back.

Soldiers walked along a line, distributing hoes, and the regiment began digging defensive earthworks to guard against a rebel counterattack from the north. As the regiment was located along the river, and Ames's division was to their east, Jim knew that the defensive line would stretch across the peninsula from the river to the ocean. This line would secure the rear of whatever force attacked Fort Fisher.

The men worked quickly through the night. The naval bombardment had driven the rebs inside and off the parapets. Otherwise, the 27th would be under constant fire.

"I wonder what them rebs is gonna think when they git up in the morning and see what us coloreds done within sight of their own big-man fort," William giggled. "Lordy!"

It didn't matter how weary everyone was. Men replaced diggers who tired and stepped back to rest, and hoes passed to the new laborers. Logs were brought in to reinforce the breastworks, now climbing higher. They kept at it long after the sun had risen on a windy, clear day, digging a deep, strong, and reinforced earthen works, raised on both sides, designed to protect them from both directions. It was deep enough for a man to stand in.

Shortly after eight o'clock, General Paine, commander of the 27th, walked along the earth works and nodded approvingly.

"Good job," he said. "Get some rest, men. We're all going to need it."

CHAPTER 16

Fort Fisher

Saturday, January 14, 1865

For the second night in a row, Caleb had not slept. The first night's failure was due to pre-battle anxiety. Tonight, the constant barrage from the ironclads made sleep impossible. At dusk the prior evening, Admiral Porter had withdrawn the Union gunboats farther offshore and given their crews the night off. However, the ironclads stayed in close, peppering the fort with shell and shot.

Beneath the walls, conditions were deteriorating. There were no comfortable quarters in which to rest. No fires could be started inside, and all they had to eat was what little they had brought from their barracks. Without access to the latrines along the river, sanitation was miserable, and the offal room was overflowing and reeked.

Men's nerves frayed. There was little conversation, and the soldiers' dust-choked coughing became more frequent.

Caleb searched the faces of the men in his crew and spoke with each about his family, loved ones, or other thoughts of home.

The only positive news was that General Whiting had been as good as his word. During the night, an additional seven hundred soldiers had been ferried across the river on the steamer *Pettaway*, bringing the garrison's complement to over fifteen hundred. Caleb feared, however, that when the land attack came, not everyone would be in condition to respond.

"There's dozens of dead or wounded," Lieutenant Pinson confided to Caleb quietly, sidling up to him in the bombproof. "We can't go outside to bury the bodies. We're just stacking them up."

Caleb nodded absently. "The guns?" he asked.

The lieutenant shook his head. "I was up top. The seaface is gone to hell. What a mess. Most guns are smashed or off their carriages, lying on their sides, useless. The top of the parapet is cratered."

"Repairs?" Caleb asked.

The lieutenant snorted in disgust. "Not with this bombardment. A single gun would take hours. And anyone sent up wouldn't last more than fifteen minutes."

"You asked me if I thought Bragg would come," Caleb said. "What do you think?"

"General Whiting has sent one telegram after another. From the top of the Northeast Bastion, we can see Yankee campfires on the beach."

"Six miles?"

"Maybe that," the lieutenant answered.

"The new men?" Caleb asked.

"A company from the First North Carolina Heavy Artillery, a company of the 10th, maybe four companies of the 40th North Carolina. About fifty sailors and marines."

"Good men?"

The lieutenant shrugged. "We'll see."

Caleb nodded. "By God, we need Bragg."

"General Whiting has gone across the river to the telegraph office at Smithville to personally take charge of the telegraph messages," the lieutenant continued. "The signaling across the river is not working with all the smoke. He fears they don't understand up in Wilmington how desperate our situation is."

Caleb shook his head.

General Whiting had counted seventy-six enemy ships and sent a messenger to signal a telegram. When the general did not receive any response, the lieutenant told Caleb that he had left to plead with Bragg more directly.

Lieutenant Fairly entered the bombproof and nodded to Caleb.

"Colonel Lamb would like your opinion on the landface batteries," he said.

Caleb gestured to Corporal Jennings, and together with the two lieutenants, the pair made their way through the underground corridor to the Northeast Bastion. They quickly climbed the outside ladder at its rear.

Colonel Lamb stood behind the sandbagged wall, next to General Whiting and his aides. The general turned to Caleb as he approached.

"It's our running sergeant," he announced warmly.

Colonel Lamb turned and nodded a greeting. The toll of sleepless nights and impending battle was visible on his face. He looked far worse than he had forty-eight hours earlier, when they had ridden to his wife's cottage.

"Can these cannons be fixed?" the general asked, gesturing back toward the landface parapet.

"I've seen the ones on my battery, General," Caleb answered. "I don't think so, sir."

The general shook his head. "I'm not worried about the seaface, Sergeant. We are well past that point. But the landface—we'll need every cannon we can fire if we're to stop the Yankee ground assault."

"These aren't my guns, General. I'm not as familiar with them as—"

"The ones whose guns they were are dead," the general said simply. "They're yours now."

"Yes, sir."

Caleb and Corporal Jennings made their way back to the parapet and turned right. Staying tight against the sandbagged outer wall, they crawled on hands and knees up and down each traverse, avoiding the craters, carefully inspecting each cannon. Yankee shells slammed into the wall and parapet around them. Caleb prayed one didn't land too close.

There was no need to speak. The damage was obvious. When they finished, they sprinted back to the Northeast Bastion and the relative safety of the outer sandbagged wall. Unlike Colonel Lamb and General Whiting, who continued to stand, Caleb felt no need to demonstrate a bravado he did not feel. He slumped down with his back against the outer wall.

"Like the seaface, it's a mess," he reported. "Most of the guns are off their mounts or damaged and can't be repaired. Many are both." The exact number was not important. It was only going to get worse.

"Can they be remounted?" the general asked.

"No, sir," Caleb answered. "That would require carpenters to build new carriages from scratch. Without a rail system, carriages can't be constructed on the ground and hoisted up. The lumber would have to be hand-carried to the emplacements, and they'd have to be built up here. Four to five hours each, even if the lumber is cut down below first."

No carpentry crew would last the time needed to build a new carriage, let alone a whole series. The men would become immediate targets of the federal fleet.

The general took a deep breath and looked toward Colonel Lamb, who did not respond. The colonel stared through a pair of binoculars toward the river side of the peninsula.

Caleb knew that the general was tempted.

"It won't work, General," Caleb said. "Even if we got new carriages up here, we'd still need a scaffold with block and tackle to lift and position each gun. We'd have to build those up here also."

It was inevitable that the cannons would all be destroyed and that the fort would have to defend itself without them.

"It'll come down to what General Bragg does," the general said. "This morning, he promised to send down a thousand of Hoke's men tonight by steamer, but only if we sent back to the other side of the river the seven hundred who got here last night."

"Send back?" Lieutenant Fairly asked.

General Whiting waved his hand dismissively. "He finally agreed to send down Hoke's men and let us keep the ones from last night. But it wasn't easy."

The general pointed toward where Colonel Lamb was looking. "General Bragg telegraphed us that, during the night, the Yankees dug an entrenchment the width of the peninsula, from ocean to river. The campfires we saw up the beach last night were a ruse. The whole damn Yankee army moved down here. Now they're dug in."

Colonel Lamb lowered his glasses. "Daisy's cottage," he said tonelessly. "Our house at Craig's Landing. There's Yankees crawling all over it. My home."

"At least your wife and children are safe, Colonel," General Whiting said.

Caleb's thoughts immediately raced to Elizabeth and his ride along the river with the colonel two days earlier. She hadn't been at the cottage. He prayed she had gotten some warning and escaped to Wilmington. He was terrified for her safety if wandering soldiers came upon her.

Elizabeth was a simple, unassuming woman, in many ways not used to the ways of the world. He hoped her naïveté would not lead her into danger.

He had experienced these same emotions during the Christmas attack and spent much of his time then worrying about her. After the Yankees left, he had raced to her cottage at his first opportunity, only to find her disconsolate. Fearing the worst, he had demanded to know if there had been some sort of attack. Although her response had made no sense to him, he had been relieved that she was safe and had survived the Yankee occupation.

Again, he experienced that same fierce desire to protect her. He did not want to imagine a future without her.

"General," Colonel Lamb announced, his glasses still trained up the river. General Whiting and his aides crowded closer to the parapet.

"I see it," the general answered.

Despite the danger, Caleb twisted around and stood. Two miles away, a steamer heading down the river had begun a slow turn to the left and was now heading toward Craig's Landing. It appeared to be intending to dock. Yankees still swarmed over the ground and landing, and as the steamer approached, they began pointing.

"It's the supply steamer *Isaac Wells*, out of Wilmington," General Whiting said.

Colonel Lamb studied the situation through his glasses. "It hasn't been down for weeks. Why is it going to Craig's Landing? It usually unloads at Battery Buchanan."

"It doesn't want to risk being targeted by the fleet," General Whiting answered. "Perhaps General Bragg sent down ammunition."

As the observers on the battery watched, the steamer slowed. The Yankees, who minutes earlier had been crawling over the landing and the Lamb cottage, disappeared from view.

"Sergeant!" Colonel Lamb barked. "Fire a warning shot to that steamer."

Caleb, Corporal Jennings, and Lieutenant Pinson leapt toward a thirty-two-pounder. The three of them turned and loaded it in less than a minute.

"Over its bow," the lieutenant commanded.

Corporal Jennings adjusted the gun's altitude as Caleb and the lieutenant lined it up. Captain Fairly had joined them and lit the botefeux. When the steamer was one hundred yards from the wharf, Corporal Jennings nodded to his sergeant. Caleb waited for the other three to crouch down before lighting the touch hole. The shot arched cleanly over the steamer's bow, splashing just beyond its port side. However, the steamer continued to head straight for the landing.

When the steamer sidled alongside the dock and tied off, blue coats emerged from every hiding place at the landing, quickly overpowering the civilian crew. The steamer and her cargo, intended for the fort, were now in Yankee hands.

"Upriver," General Whiting said, and the group's collective eyes swung northward. The Confederate gunboat *Chickamauga* had been trailing the steamer and had apparently seen what had transpired. The gunboat swung in toward the landing. Before Yankee soldiers could remove any of the *Isaac Wells's* cargo, the *Chickamauga* unleashed a broadside, blasting holes in the side of the supply steamer. Within seconds, it had settled at the bottom of the river, still tied to the dock.

"At least the Yankees won't get any of our powder," Corporal Jennings said grimly.

The colonel shook his head disconsolately. "That is not the important point," he said. "General Bragg sent that steamer down to Craig's Landing to resupply the fort. How in control is he if he doesn't know that Craig's Landing has been in Yankee hands this whole day?"

CHAPTER 17

Federal Point, Fort Fisher

January 14, 1865

The six oarsmen expertly guided the small cutter toward the shore. Just before the spot where the waves started to break, the cutter hesitated, the sailors studying the swirling eddies. On command, the oarsmen increased their stroke, driving the small boat as far up the sand as possible before grounding it. As it tipped to one side, two oarsmen jumped out, as did the lone passenger dressed in a colonel's uniform.

As the sailors turned the boat around in the surf, the colonel waded ashore. Colonel Newton Curtis walked to the water's edge and extended his hand. "Colonel Comstock, welcome back to Federal Point."

After shaking his host's hand, Colonel Cyrus Comstock attempted to wring the water from his clothes.

"Come, Colonel," Curtis invited, extending a guiding hand, "there is a fire to dry your clothing."

The pair walked up the beach, and Cyrus Comstock draped his shoes and socks over a grate adjacent to a smoky campfire.

"General Terry is waiting down near the fort," Colonel Curtis said. "We can get close to the landface. The rebels have been driven off both walls."

Colonel Comstock looked up sharply but said nothing.

Newton called over a soldier and obtained dry breeches for his friend. After Comstock finished changing, the pair struck out down the peninsula.

By training, Colonel Cyrus Comstock was an engineer. A Massachusetts native, he had been assigned to the Army Corps of Engineers upon graduation from West Point in 1855. When the War of the Rebellion broke out, he had been instrumental in designing the fortifications and defenses around Washington. During the Siege of Vicksburg in 1863, he had served as chief engineer in General Ulysses Grant's Army of Tennessee. His siege-planning had helped ensure the city's fall to Union forces on July 4. His plans and incisive engineering analysis of the rebels' defenses had won the admiration of General Grant, and in the fall of 1864, he had been appointed General Grant's senior aide-de-camp.

When the first Fort Fisher expedition was planned, Grant had made sure to include Comstock and ordered that he accompany the force to render his analysis of the fort. That command decision resulted in Cyrus Comstock and Newton Curtis spending Christmas night in that rifle pit.

Five hundred yards north of the landface, the pair spotted General Terry and his aides, surveying the fort. Comstock and Curtis hurried to join them. One of General Terry's aides, Captain George Towle, took binoculars from his belt and handed them to the general. Alfred Terry studied the fort wordlessly before lowering them and turning to the two colonels.

"How many field pieces were on the wall in December?" he asked.

"Sixteen," Colonel Comstock answered without hesitation.

"There are nine there now," General Terry said. "The rest have been knocked out by the bombardment. What's your opinion of the traverses?"

Colonel Comstock studied the fortification carefully. "They appear to be heavily cratered. It will be difficult for rebel infantry to maintain a direct line of fire on us once we gain the first traverse."

General Terry nodded. "That goes both ways. We'll be hampered by those same craters."

The general lifted the field glasses and swung them side to side, perusing the length of the wall. "Any attackers coming down along the ocean side will be exposed to fire from infantry atop the length of the wall."

"That's true, General," Comstock said, "and the land in the middle is marsh. But on the river side, the land slopes down near the water's edge. Infantry advancing down that way would still come under fire from rifles along the western edge but would be screened from rebels at the eastern edge of the wall."

"The key then," Curtis interjected, "is to have at least a feint along the ocean side to keep the rebels on the wall from moving to the western side and concentrating fire on our forces there."

"And those men would be you and your brigade," the general said, turning to Curtis. "You had the lead at Christmas. God knows, you wanted to go. Your brigade deserves to have the lead again, despite what your own division commander says."

"Sir?" Colonel Curtis asked.

General Terry snickered. "It's no secret that your own division commander is seeking to replace you. Just this morning, General Ames asked me again. I told him, in no uncertain words, that your New Yorkers were ready to go three weeks ago, and you would lead again."

"Thank you, sir."

"How would you do it?" the general asked.

"We'd strike from down along the river's edge," Curtis answered, pointing. "We'd cross that wooden bridge. It's not very wide, and its flooring is mostly gone. The rebs may yet blow it up. The men would have to pass the bridge on both sides, through the marsh. It'll be tough going, but they can get through the marsh. Then, there's those palisades the rebs have built. What we can't blow down with cannon, we'll chop with axes.

"I say we attack in waves," Curtis continued, "since it'll be a narrow battle line. My own brigade first, then the rest of the division—Bell's New Hampshire brigade and Pennypacker's Pennsylvanians. We could even use the coloreds, if need be. They fight well, and the Lord knows they want to."

"Maybe," General Terry mused, "but I need them to protect the rear. I expect Hoke to attack from the north once we are engaged against the fort. And good work, Colonel, ascertaining that it was Hoke up the peninsula. The rebel prisoners confirmed it."

"Yes, sir," Colonel Curtis answered.

"Aside from the wall, what about the readiness in the fort itself?" the general asked.

"There were eight hundred fifty soldiers stationed there," Curtis answered. "They landed another six to nine hundred last night from across the river on a steamer. They may try to add some of Hoke's men down there as well. We'll need the fleet to attack the steamers and drive them off."

The general nodded. "Munitions?"

"Possibly three thousand rounds. There's been no recent supply. They weren't expecting us till spring."

Terry nodded again. "Well, let's hope they're wrong about everything else too."

Terry handed the binoculars back to Towle, who replaced them in his belt pouch.

"I will review all this with Admiral Porter tonight," the general said with finality. "I still want the navy to disable those last nine guns and blow this palisade apart. But tomorrow, no matter what, I will have those three brigades attack along the river, with you in the lead. We won't be getting any stronger, but Bragg might."

General Terry turned and, together with his aides, began walking back up the Wilmington Road. Colonels Curtis and Comstock stepped in behind them. Just before Craig's Landing, the general and his aides turned right for the ocean and the general's meeting with Admiral Porter aboard the *Malvern*. Around them, the 27th was still digging in, improving their defensive line by the hour.

The two colonels watched the group of officers walk off. When they were out of earshot, Cyrus Comstock spun on his friend.

"You've seen her, haven't you?" he demanded.

Newton Curtis considered feigning ignorance at the question, but Cyrus's piercing stare warned him that he would be unsuccessful. The colonel would know he was lying.

Newton swallowed and looked away. "Yes," he admitted. "I've seen her."

"And she told you all this—the number of soldiers, the ammunition figures, how they plan to reinforce," Comstock said, waving his arm back toward the fort while not taking his eyes off Curtis. "Even about Hoke being up the peninsula."

"Yes, she did."

"Everything you just told General Terry, you learned from her. And you repeated it without any hesitation, word for word, because deep down you know it's true. Every word of it."

"Yes," Curtis repeated again. "I know it's reliable. Every word of it."

Comstock shook his head. "By God, Newton, what a woman!" he said, unable to hide his admiration.

Curtis looked at his friend. There was more than appreciation in his expression.

"Where is she?" Comstock begged. "I want to hear it myself."

Newton Curtis pointed up the Wilmington Road. "Her cottage is up there, maybe two miles, at most. The rebels are at least another three miles above that. But if you go," Curtis warned, "take some of these coloreds with you. Just in case."

CHAPTER 18

Confederate Point
January 14, 1865

"Asa King is dead."

"Are you sure?" Robert Dearborn asked.

"Sure as shootin," Seth said. "We gave them a heck of a fight. There was three regiments of Yankees, maybe more. We moved back through the woods, trying to slow them up, and Asa, he couldn't keep up."

"I heard there was only skirmishers, and you fellas skedaddled—ran like hell, they say," a soldier in the rear said.

"Who says that?" Seth demanded, turning to the rear of the column and walking backwards, his musket bouncing on his shoulder.

"I said it," the soldier repeated. "Everyone's talking. Heard y'all left Asa on his own. He the only one stayed there fighting."

"How do you know he's dead?" Robert asked, drawing Seth's attention back to the front. "Maybe he's just captured."

"Quiet down, you two," a sergeant said. "We're getting closer."

The 66th was on the move again. After his encounter with the doubting major in the woods the day before, Seth had made it back up the peninsula to where the 66th was encamped. There had been no reinforcement for the Confederate skirmishers who had approached the Yankee-covered beach. The 66th had waited the rest of the day for orders to advance, but they never came.

Today had been different. A soldier had spotted General Braxton Bragg near the front.

"Looks like he done left Sugar Loaf," Jebediah Smith said as he cleaned his musket.

"Something will be happening soon," Seth agreed.

Shortly thereafter, a lieutenant raced through the encampment, getting everyone on their feet and the 66th moving. They were going to attack the Yankees, believed to still be on the beach.

"General Bragg is here himself," said a soldier in front of Seth. "We'll drive them right into the ocean. See if Yankees can swim."

A mile north of the Yankee landing zone, at the tip of Myrtle Sound, the lieutenant directed everyone into a line of attack. He dispatched skirmishers forward to protect the battle line.

Seth and Robert crawled forward. Before the Confederate skirmishers reached the spot of yesterday's debacle, they spotted Abbott's brigade, well entrenched behind a stand of pines. Yankee regimental flags flapped atop the earth and log breastworks that guarded the Union landing zone. The wind was starting to pick up, and the flags tugged hard at their poles.

"You think they spotted us?" Robert asked.

"They know we're here," Seth answered.

There was nothing to do but wait. The location of the enemy was sent back to the rear, and the attacking force would soon be fully positioned. *Perhaps a flanking plan*, Seth thought. He figured he had about an hour before the battle began.

Just behind the Yankee fortification was where Asa had been killed the day before. Seth wondered whether the Yankees had enough Christian decency to bury his friend and whether a preacher had officiated.

He had known Asa for over a year, since joining the 66th. Seth, Asa, and Robert had become inseparable. Some of the older veterans had advised against such a thing, but Seth had ignored the warnings.

And now Asa was dead.

He wouldn't be dead, of course, if those damn Yankees hadn't thought they could tell his people what to do, if they didn't insist on coming down to North Carolina. He wouldn't be dead if the Yankees hadn't known that they were coming and set a trap for them.

Seth didn't doubt that they had set a trap. Those hadn't been pickets in the woods or even a skirmish line. He regretted his statement to his comrades that that's all they were.

Asa had known better. As soon as the false bravado was out of Seth's mouth, Asa had scoffed. There had been two regiments of federals in the woods, waiting.

Asa could have retreated. After all, the captain had. Everyone else did too. Why hadn't Asa?

Seth had seen the same captain last night, sitting around another cook fire. Neither had looked at the other.

"I have to pee," Seth said.

Several soldiers away from him, Benjamin Cutler rolled up onto his left side. "So do I," he said.

"Not here," Robert said. "The Yankees will shoot you in the butt if you drop your trousers."

The men around them snickered.

"I have to drop one myself," Robert added.

"There's a spot behind that poplar stand," the sergeant said. "The land curves down and is sheltered. Don't take all day. And just the three of you," he added quickly when several other soldiers twisted around.

The trio squirmed around the other way and crawled back until the terrain dropped off. They rose to a crouch and moved west, away from the ocean.

"I have to fill my canteen," Robert said.

"There's a stream we passed on the way up," Benjamin said.

The three trudged along, hunting for a good spot. They kept a vigilant eye to the south, hoping to avoid a Yankee sharpshooter targeting easy prey.

"Where's that stream?" Seth demanded.

"I was sure it was back here. No. Maybe just over above that stand," Benjamin answered, switching directions and breaking into a trot through the underbrush. Robert and Seth hustled to catch up. Benjamin changed directions again.

"You don't know where it is," Robert accused.

Instead of answering, Benjamin paused on top of a sandy crest and pointed down. "That's a good spot."

"For water?" Seth asked, seeing no stream.

"To take a pee."

"I'll go first," Seth said. "Someone should guard."

After relieving himself, he climbed back up the knoll. Robert went next into the depression and searched for a suitable bush.

Seth studied the terrain. Their walk had brought them close to the river. Through the trees, Seth made out the lighter area of a clearing. In the middle sat a whitewashed cottage, smoke curling from a chimney.

Robert returned, and Benjamin went next down to the hollow.

Seth reached out and grabbed Robert's arm.

"What in blazes—?" Robert asked, pulling back.

"Shut up," Seth hissed and pulled his fellow soldier to the ground with him. Through the clearing, Seth saw the blur of a Yankee uniform. The man carried no rifle. An officer. Four black soldiers holding rifles strolled leisurely into view.

"There's nigger Yankees over there."

"Huh?" Robert asked. Scampering to his knees, he craned his neck.

"There's a white Yankee officer in that clearing with nigger soldiers," Seth repeated.

The Union officer stood by himself. The black soldiers gestured and talked with each other. Directly behind the soldiers stood a small paddock and horse shed. As Seth watched, a woman entered his field of vision and began conversing with the officer. The black soldiers lounged about, paying no attention. From the way she greeted him, it was apparent that the officer and the woman knew each other.

Benjamin returned. "I am done," he said.

"Shut up," Seth barked. "There's Yankees. Let's go."

Instead of moving, Benjamin leaned off to one side and stared straight ahead. "Where?" he asked.

"You keep yapping, they'll be right damn here," Seth said.

He stood, hunchbacked, turned, and headed straight down the back of the rise. At the bottom, he began double-timing back toward his unit. The other two hurried after him. Robert caught up with Seth.

"They ain't following us, what's your hurry?" he asked.

Without slowing, Seth turned. "Did you see that?" he demanded. "Did you see what I saw?"

Robert nodded. "Yeah, a white officer with his nigger soldiers. Could be them that was outside Petersburg. But they ain't following us."

"Not the niggers, stupid, the horse! Did you see it?"

"They got cavalry?" Robert asked.

"Don't be a fool!" Seth spat. "That ain't no social call. The chestnut horse with the star on its forehead! The woman!"

When Robert looked at him blankly, Seth shook his head in disgust. "You really are stupid," he said. "She was talking to the Yankee officer. I seen that woman and that horse. Yesterday, up in Wilmington. Watched us as we formed up in the morning."

"Yeah, so?" Robert asked. If he was offended by Seth again calling him stupid, he didn't show it.

"Yesterday, the Yankees knew we was coming. She ain't just a horse-riding woman. She's a goddamn, yellow-bellied Yankee spy. She's the one told them we was coming. She's the one that got Asa killed."

Robert opened his mouth but said nothing.

Hearing crashing through the woods, the three dropped to the ground. When a gray line appeared out of the brush, they stood back up. It was their unit.

"Where we all going now?" Benjamin asked.

The sergeant answered. "We've been pulled back. Again. Word is that General Bragg decided not to attack. We're heading back up the peninsula."

CHAPTER 19

Fort Fisher

Sunday, January 15, 1865

Just after midnight

Lieutenant Pinson was awakened by a rough shaking of his shoulder. He was surprised that he had fallen asleep, given the constant Yankee barrage. *You can get used to most anything,* he thought.

Lieutenant Fairly, one of General Whiting's aides, was leaning over him.

"The general and colonel say General Bragg will attack the Yankees from the north before morning. They want to deploy troops from here up the peninsula to trap the Yankees between the two lines."

Lieutenant Pinson rubbed his eyes and sat up. Around him, men beneath Mound Battery were slumbering or just sitting quietly. A shell slammed into the wall, and the ground shook. He estimated that strike to have been two hundred yards north of where he sat.

"Bragg is going to attack tonight?" he asked.

Lieutenant Fairly stood back up straight. "That's what the general and colonel assume is his plan."

Daniel Pinson didn't know Lieutenant Fairly, having just met him on Friday at Battery Buchanan when he landed with General Whiting and Major Hill. But he believed Fairly, like Major Hill and the general, to be a good man. None of them had to come down to the fort. They could have stayed in Wilmington for this battle, which is where they were assigned. In fact, he realized, coming down without orders risked a court martial.

Lieutenant Pinson stood and stretched his back and legs.

"That's a big assumption, Lieutenant. Any word from General Bragg's headquarters at Sugar Loaf that they are planning to attack? Telegram, signal, messenger?"

He tried to keep his tone from becoming confrontational. This was not the young lieutenant's fault.

"The Yankees have to attack today," Fairly said. "They've moved down the peninsula. They can't just sit there in the cold marsh. They must be concerned about General Bragg sending General Hoke's division. It has to be today."

Lieutenant Pinson nodded absently. Left unsaid was that, if General Bragg was going to send Hoke to attack, it would best be at night—when the Union fleet could not target the Confederates easily and when signaling between spotters on the peninsula and shipboard gunners would be hampered.

"What's the plan?" Pinson asked.

"The colonel wants to put ten companies just outside the fort, with skirmishers above. As soon as General Hoke strikes south, we'll attack from this end. The Yankees won't be able to get accurate fire from the fleet on us, so we'll be on equal terms."

"But has General Bragg actually ordered an attack tonight?" Pinson pressed.

"General Whiting sent a message to Sugar Loaf requesting an immediate attack," Fairly replied.

"And?"

"He hasn't heard back yet."

Daniel Pinson sighed. "There'll be seven, eight, nine thousand Yankees, and we can only send a few hundred from the fort. We can't support them from the landface. The fleet will target that, even in the darkness."

Lieutenant Pinson belted on his revolver and sword. Grabbing his hat, he followed Lieutenant Fairly through the bombproof. Along the corridors, sergeants were waking the men. Soldiers crowded beneath the Northeast Bastion, quietly checking their weapons and ammunition. There was not the usual pre-battle grumbling, and Lieutenant Pinson wondered whether it was the relief of finally being able to do more than just cower beneath the walls.

The line of soldiers wound back through the tunnel, and the pair pushed past them. Colonel Lamb stood at the front of the line. When he saw the two junior officers, he moved back to them.

"We're short of lieutenants," Colonel Lamb said to Pinson. "Can you serve with Company H tonight?"

Lieutenant Pinson agreed.

More men arrived beneath the battery and in the corridors, and Colonel Lamb called for the soldiers of Company H to come forward with their commander, Captain Patterson. When the colonel got the company arranged at the front, he led the unit, single file, out of the bombproof into the rear yard. Lieutenant Pinson stayed at the rear to hurry stragglers. The line snaked right and stayed tight against the wall. They double-timed their way to the sally port in the middle of the landface. There were still two twelve-pound Napoleons remaining in the protected sally port, and their crews stood by them silently.

The gate to the sally port opened, and Colonel Lamb and Captain Patterson led the men out. They turned right toward the ocean. Proceeding by the light of the moon, Company H moved quietly through the palisade. Once above the stockade, the men lay down on their stomachs, and the company crawled north and east toward the beach, searching for Yankee pickets. The location of the enemy army had to be established.

One hundred yards from the beach, Lieutenant Pinson spotted a lone sentry, outlined against the moonlight. He waved a hush to his left. The signal was conveyed down the line, but one man shouted "Quiet!" too loudly, and the Yankee sentry ducked down and out of sight. Seconds later, musket fire rang out from the Yankee ranks.

"Get the line back!" Colonel Lamb ordered. "We'll set up by the depression in front of the palisade."

Already, some soldiers were returning the Yankee fire, and Lieutenant Pinson stood and raced along the rear of the line, ordering everyone to stop firing. Together with Captain Patterson, they backed the company to more protected terrain.

Colonel Lamb slid down next to Lieutenant Pinson.

"Go back and tell the others where the Yankee pickets are. They won't attack in the dark, but their skirmishers will keep up a steady fire. Get the men deployed in a line just behind us and have them dig in. When we hear battle sounds from the north, we'll attack."

Lieutenant Pinson moved back through the palisade and through the sally port. He prayed that one of his own jittery sentries didn't shoot him as he approached. Once inside the fort, he relayed the colonel's instructions, and the other nine companies moved out to their assigned positions. Back above the palisade, captains kept arranging and rearranging the companies into attack formations.

Each man used his bayonet to scrape out a defensive rifle pit. The men lay flat, their rifles held in front of them. They waited, straining for the sounds of battle.

After nearly four hours, Lieutenant Pinson knew that General Bragg was not going to attack that night. He also knew that the Yankees would attack the next day. With the protection of darkness gone, his soldiers' best chance of attacking the federal troops on Confederate Point had slipped away.

When dawn broke, Colonel Lamb returned with Company H from their forward line and ordered everyone to withdraw back to the fort. Lieutenant Pinson was not surprised.

CHAPTER 20

A human chain of sailors passed crates up from the hold and across the *Iosco's* deck to her port side. The pile of boxes at the end of the chain climbed higher. A boom and tackle was positioned against the rail, and crates were carefully lowered from the deck pile down into the ship's launch. Sailors in the launch positioned and balanced each new crate as it arrived.

There was no wind, and the sea was calm. There was no roll to the ship. The sky was clear, and the temperature hovered just above freezing.

Conditions were perfect for naval artillery, and the Union was taking full advantage.

The *Iosco* was anchored at the southern end of the line of gunboats, closest to shore in front of Fort Fisher. As the federal army had been redeployed down the peninsula two days earlier, the navy's lines of gunboats had been shortened accordingly. The fifty-nine warships were arrayed in three separate lines, running from Mound Battery to just a mile north of the landface. A fourth line of ships was positioned in reserve behind the main three. Five ironclads were anchored in front of the three battle lines of gunboats.

The *Iosco's* battle line continued to shell the seaface—more to keep rebel gunners from harassing the fleet than to destroy cannons—while the balance of the navy's gunboats pounded the landface. The gunboats' rate of fire was the heaviest it had been in the three days of bombardment. Every gun on the *Iosco* was firing.

From the bow, Patrick watched as the *Iosco's* launch filled with crates.

"I hope they don't forget our revolvers," Seamus mused next to him.

Patrick didn't answer. He'd had a sick feeling in his stomach since rolling out of his hammock at four a.m. He hadn't been assigned to the engine room that morning—the whole shore party had been excused from their usual shipboard duties—and he had tarried at breakfast while the fleet maneuvered into battle lines. At seven fifteen, the *New Ironsides* had fired the first shot of the day, and the cacophony of naval artillery had commenced.

The previous two days' firing had been selective, covering the landing zone or targeting specific artillery pieces on the walls. Now, it was a general, massive pounding, intended to destroy the fortifications as well as the palisade in front of the landface. That would ease the infantry assault.

No matter how much pounding the fleet inflicted, Patrick expected that, before the day was over, he'd be facing the defenders of that fort with a revolver in one hand and a cutlass in the other. The captain had left him no option.

"The men like you," he had said.

Patrick questioned whether he should have concentrated more on keeping the men from liking him. At least Seamus seemed comfortable with his assignment. But Seamus supported the war. Patrick knew that his older friend would not try to avoid going ashore.

Then there was Nat, who wanted to go ashore but had been denied permission. Well, Nat had a personal motive, too.

Maybe, if Patrick had been offered the chance to attack the British Parliament with cutlasses, he might have volunteered. But he had no quarrel with the rebels. He had only been in America six years, and he had never been down South. Why was this to be his fight? He could have migrated to Canada, like the Tobins from his hometown had before him, but he had chosen New York. In hindsight, a bad choice, he decided.

Patrick and Seamus wended their way back to the boom. Many on the shore party were crowding about, watching their supplies be lowered and positioned. John Barber, the Captain of the Hold, was helping direct the loading, even though he had volunteered for the shore attack. Jake Rowley, Billy Preston, James Madison—Patrick counted the volunteers, one by one.

Nat was there too. He and Sven had finished their shift with Jason Cullinane, serving as fireman. As he and Seamus approached the group, Patrick read the disappointment and longing in his friend's eyes.

A sailor, lifting an awkward long box with a round top, lost his footing on a ladder step and dropped the crate. It burst open. Hoes and shovels tumbled out.

"What's this?" Seaman Vranken demanded.

"We'll be doing digging," Ensign Feilberg answered. "We'll trench a series of rifle pits leading up to the fort. Places for you men to jump into and hide as you advance between rebel volleys."

"Digging?" Patrick asked. He looked hard at Nat.

"Yes, Sheedy, digging," Feilberg answered. "You'll be happy to have a place to tuck your head and your arse when rebel shot and shell comes a-flying."

"Iffin' it's digging we be needing, then we need our best diggers onshore. Ain't that so, Ensign?" Patrick asked.

"Of course it is, Sheedy. You'll need to put your backs into it. It won't be all glory on there."

"Then why not take the best shovel man on this boat?" Patrick demanded, pointing at Nat. "He's the best digger by far. I've seen it with me own eyes, every day for nigh a year."

The ensign's eyes moved from the coal heaver to his fireman and back again.

Seamus jumped in. "Aye, Ensign, it be true. Nat here is the best coal heaver aboard, ask any of the firemen. He's got that big, strong, black back that never tires. He's a legend in the engine room."

"The captain already approved the forty-three to go," the ensign argued, but Patrick saw doubt creeping onto the officer's face.

"So what?" Patrick pressed. "If we need deep holes to stay alive, then we be needing the best diggers there are."

The surrounding sailors began grumbling as the idea took hold in them.

"That's right," Seaman Vranken spoke up. "It's our lives. Let the nigger go. We need him."

"But the report—" the ensign objected.

"Damn your report!" Seamus shouted. "The nigger deserves to go. He's earned it. And God knows he has a cause to be going. Davis, you still want a part of this?"

Nat Davis elbowed his way to the front of the other sailors. Patrick was almost embarrassed to see the tears in his eyes.

"Please," was all the contraband said.

Ensign Feilberg still hesitated, but the surrounding grumbling intensified, and the circle tightened around the officer.

"Alright," Feilberg finally announced, as if to ward off a mutiny. "I can change it. I'll fix it with the captain. Davis, you're number forty-four. Now, let's finish loading these boats and climb aboard. It's time to shove off."

Fort Fisher

Caleb could tell his lieutenant had had a rough night. His uniform was caked with dirt and soaked through. He had made no effort to clean off the mud.

"We went out last night," he explained as Caleb approached. "Waited all night for General Bragg."

Caleb didn't have to ask what happened.

"What about Hoke's men?" he asked. "The thousand?"

The lieutenant's eyes appeared glassy. *He's sensing defeat,* Caleb reasoned.

"They left downriver in steamers. One got stuck on a sandbar. Had to transfer the men. Then another got stuck . . ." His voice trailed off.

"Any?"

"Maybe two hundred made it. South Carolinians."

Caleb nodded. "They can try again today. How're the walls?"

"Maybe three or four cannons left on the seaface, for what good that'll do us."

"And the landface?" Caleb asked.

"Just that thirty-two-pounder you fired at the steamer yesterday and one Columbiad. And whatever is left in the sally port. I think two field pieces."

"We just need more men," Caleb said, trying to sound optimistic.

The lieutenant moved past Caleb without looking at him.

Confederate Point

Seth Colburn rolled onto his back and brushed the dirt off the front of his uniform. Now that the sun was up, there would be no attack. The Yankee fleet would decimate any rebel force in daylight. He and his fellows had lain in the sand all night, muskets at the ready. He'd been sure that an order would come to advance and that he would be springing to his feet and charging in the moonlight. On several occasions, he'd heard musket fire from the direction of the fort and thought the battle might be starting.

But the order never came.

Now it was time for breakfast.

CHAPTER 21

Federal Point, North Carolina
Sunday, January 15, 1865
Noon

Two miles north of Fort Fisher, eighteen hundred Union sailors milled about on the beach. They conversed, laughed, and prayed. The enlisted men were dressed in their blue, double-breasted sailor jackets, and most sported the blue, "round-boy" sailor hats, many of them jammed low at a jaunty angle.

Seamus was having trouble keeping the *Iosco's* men together. With only forty-four sailors, the *Iosco's* contribution to the attack force was one of the fleet's smallest. Some of the larger ships had as many as two hundred volunteers. Seamus kept calling out to men who wandered off when they spotted acquaintances from other ships.

Officers were decked out in their braided greatcoats. Off to the side in the scrub was a contingent of marines, each identifiable by the Sharps carbine he carried. In contrast, every sailor carried a holstered Colt revolver, with a boarding cutlass slung at his side.

"Where are the lead officers?" Patrick asked.

Seamus gestured inland, toward a group of braided officers who huddled around Fleet Captain Breese.

"It's a bit late to be deciding strategy, wouldn't you say?" Patrick groused.

Occasionally, one of the sailors on the beach would turn toward the fort, whose ominous walls were in full view, and shout.

"We're coming for you, Johnny Reb!" was a common refrain, almost always punctuated with peals of laughter from the sailors surrounding the shouter.

"The lads are nervous," Seamus observed.

Patrick stood on his toes and craned his neck. Unsatisfied, he climbed the incline at the edge of the beach and stood atop the grassy plain.

"I can't see our ensigns," he called down.

Ensign Jameson appeared with the Iosco's master-at-arms, Joseph Hinkelman.

"Davis, you're a heaver. Grab a shovel!" Jameson commanded. He indicated the pile of spades stacked at the water's edge. "Go with Hinkelman to the front. Report to Lieutenant Preston and dig breastworks for the marines to use for cover as we advance."

Ensign Jameson looked about. "You too Barber, Vranken, Phillips."

Patrick studied his coal heaver as the contraband hefted a spade. A pang of guilt overcame him.

"We'll go," he yelled to Ensign Jameson.

When the officer looked up, Seamus repeated Patrick's offer.

"Alright then," Jameson said. "Flanagan, Sheedy. That makes seven. Go with the master-at-arms and dig wherever the lieutenant tells you."

Patrick and Seamus walked to the water's edge and hefted two spades.

Turning to Ensign Jameson, Seamus jerked his thumb over his shoulder.

"What's the plan?" he asked. "We're supposed to help with the men, keep them in line, but there doesn't seem to be any need now, does there?"

The other four crewmen from the Iosco were already following the master-at-arms down the sand toward the fort. The naval artillery still pounded the landface, and from where he stood, Patrick could not see any rebels on the parapets.

Ensign Jameson approached them. "They think most of the cannons on this side of the fort are destroyed," he said. "The rebels are off the walls. You should be alright to dig."

"For how long?" Seamus asked.

"When they're sure the guns are gone off the wall, the shelling will stop. The ships will blow a long whistle as a signal to attack. Colonel Curtis's men will charge up the other side along the road, cross the wooden bridge, and go through the fort's open end by the river. Once they're on top of the first traverse, we will charge from this side, get through the palisade, and then climb that grassy slope to that bastion that sticks out at the corner. It'll be all hand-to-hand fighting. We'll have the advantage with cutlasses and revolvers. The rebs will only have single-shot muskets. This is the type of fighting us sailors train for."

Seamus looked from his ensign to the fort and back again.

"These men haven't trained for anything," Seamus said evenly. "You're saying we're to attack in a line along the shore, one behind the other?"

"The center of the peninsula is too marshy," Jameson replied.

Patrick saw the other five sailors from the *Iosco* getting farther ahead of them, joining sailors from other ships who had also been sent forward to dig.

"Then what?" Patrick asked.

"The marines will dig in as close to the fort as they can get and provide cover for our attack. The sailors will advance in three waves. When the last wave passes, the marines will follow them in, providing cover to keep the rebels off the wall. We're to climb that wall and take the cannons and then fan out across the yard."

Patrick looked back at the sailors milling about on the beach. Two sailors lifted a third in a handstand over their heads. When he tumbled to the ground, pulling the other two with him, the sailors standing around them broke out in a raucous jeer.

"What about us?" Seamus asked.

"You'll have time to get back here before the whistles blow. Or you can wait until the line reaches you and then fall in with the marines at the back."

Two groups of sailors had found a length of rope and were engaging in a tug of war.

"C'mon, Patrick," Seamus said. "We best be going."

The pair struck out after their shipmates. They trotted to catch up.

Six hundred yards from the fort, Lieutenant Preston stopped the group and arranged them in a line parallel with the fort's landface. They began digging. The lieutenant sent some sailors back to the pines for fallen logs that they dragged forward and added to the rising breastworks.

When the construction of the fortification was almost completed, the lieutenant ordered two additional forward rifle pits dug parallel with the breastworks. The seven *Iosco* sailors were sent to dig the pit closest to the fort. Patrick estimated that they were now less than two hundred yards from the palisade.

The naval shelling continued to slam the landface, and Patrick could still see no rebels atop the wall. However, an occasional stray bullet whizzed into the ground behind him, kicking up sand and proving his eyesight was not reliable.

"There's a few brave lads up there," John Barber said.

"Keep your head down, men," Hinkelman warned.

Patrick got on his knees and dug with his spade, hoping his constricted posture presented a smaller target.

In half an hour, they had dug a trench two feet deep. Patrick swung the spade as fast as he could. The deeper he got the trench, the more protected he felt. An occasional bullet slammed in behind him. Patrick assumed that the shooters were targeting the diggers until he spotted the marines racing toward them from the rear. When the marines reached his position, they dove into the pits and down behind the breastworks.

"Are you men all?" Patrick asked one who tumbled next to him.

"Just the first group," the marine rasped. He paused to catch his breath. "We're under the command of Lieutenant Fagan, right over there," he said, indicating. "There'll be about four hundred of us altogether, but most of us haven't made it to shore yet."

"Haven't made it to shore?" Seamus exclaimed from the opposite end of the trench, pausing in his digging. "I thought the battle's about to begin."

"We need to get down here in position first," the marine said.

Seamus looked over at Patrick but said nothing. The pair resumed their digging, at times scraping sand out of the hole with their hands. The marine rolled onto his knees, pulled out his bayonet, and joined in.

Another round of musket fire from the wall preceded a second line of marines, who dove into the newly constructed trenches. They conferred before striking out with an officer toward the fort. One hundred fifty yards from the landface, they flattened down and began carving out yet another pit. They had no spades and used their bayonets.

That'll take a while, Patrick thought.

"Those boys be getting pretty close to them rebs," Nat said. "Lordy!"

"The men are moving!" another sailor called out. Keeping his head down, Patrick turned as the horde of sailors up the beach slowly started moving down toward the fort.

"Looks like they're going to stay real close to the water's edge," he said to Seamus. "There's some protection from the slope of the beach."

"It'll be a narrower line," Seamus answered, "when they charge."

Two couriers zigzagged amid rebel fire, flopping into the pit just to the rear of the *Iosco* sailors. Although he could not make out the words, Patrick could tell they were having an animated discussion with their officer behind the breastworks. A messenger rose up and sprinted into Patrick's trench.

"Change of plans," he huffed. "You're to stop digging and relocate over at the beach. You're to dig the rifle pits over there for the advancing sailors."

"In the name of Christ!" Seamus exclaimed, throwing down his spade in disgust. "Is there no one who knows what in hell they're doing?"

"Look," the sailor said defensively, "this is what I was told to tell you. There's better protection behind the rise this side of the beach. It's low tide, so the sand is wide. The sailors will come down tight along the grass, where there'll be more protection. They'll need pits over there."

The first marine to arrive in Patrick's pit stopped digging with his bayonet and rolled onto his back.

"Are ye daft, man?" he demanded. "Look at that terrain. If we move to the left, the closest we can dig is maybe six hundred yards from the fort. Look at those marines," he said, pointing straight ahead. "We've got pits here less than a hundred fifty yards from the enemy. And ye want us to go back to the beach, farther away?"

When the sailor didn't answer, the marine rolled back onto his stomach.

"Ah, to hell with ye," he said.

Crawling first to his knees, he grabbed his carbine and raced forward to the pit in front of him, dodging shots from the wall's sharpshooters.

In the breastworks behind them, sailors picked up their shovels and began dashing in ones and twos to the left. Patrick watched the marine who had just left his own pit conferring with his brethren. They rose as one and also raced left, toward the beach.

Directly ahead, the fort's sally port gate opened. Six Confederates rushed two field artillery pieces out the gate, just feet past the mouth of the entrance.

"Those cannons are going to open up," Seamus said.

"Men, we have to go with everyone else," Joseph Hinkelman commanded. "Grab your shovels, and let's move it!"

More sand kicked up around the rifle pit.

"Now!" Hinkelman screamed. Grabbing his spade, the master-at-arms edged to the far left side of the trench and climbed out. He ran toward the ocean. John Barber jumped out after him. Landsmen Vranken and Phillips scrambled to the edge.

Patrick was reaching for his own spade when he heard the rebel cannon's boom from the sally port. He turned to see John Barber stumble in mid stride and pitch forward headfirst, landing in a grotesque heap. Blood poured out of him in every direction, and Patrick saw, with sickening finality, that the top half of John Barber's head was gone.

Seamus moved quickly, grabbing Vranken, who was half out of the trench, and dragged him back down on top of himself.

Patrick couldn't move. He stared at the body of his shipmate fallen in the sand, a mass of red. He was dimly aware of Nat squatting next to him, reaching out and turning his shoulder away from the sight.

"Don't look, boss," he said. "He be gone to Jesus."

Patrick knew he was going to throw up. He leaned on his hands and knees and retched into the sand. Off to the side, Vranken cursed at Seamus, screaming that they had to get out of there, but the older sailor refused to let go until Vranken quieted.

Patrick flopped back against the sand wall and wiped a sleeve across his mouth.

"What happened to Hinkelman?" he asked no one in particular.

"He done made it," Nat said. "Kept going."

Patrick nodded. He never should have volunteered for this. He should have told his captain no. He knew exactly how Vranken, now lying quietly in the trench, felt. Landsman Phillips squatted next to him, peeking over the sand toward the fort.

"They've stopped," Phillips said.

"What? Who has?" Patrick asked weakly.

"The shelling's stopped," Phillips repeated.

He was right. The navy's guns were silent. From the direction of the fleet came the shriek of a single steam whistle, immediately joined by a rising crescendo as every other ship joined in.

From behind him at the fort, a corresponding human shriek erupted as rebel soldiers poured forth from wherever they had been hiding and filled the parapets.

Seamus raised his head above ground. Patrick scrambled next to him and did the same. Along the beach, he made out the top half of a blue mass as it lurched, herd-like, toward the fort. The rebel yell from the wall swelled in volume.

Seamus spun from his crouched position and looked to the river.

"This isn't right," he said. "They ain't supposed to go till the army gets on top of that wall."

"It be too late for that," Nat said. "There ain't no stopping the boys now."

CHAPTER 22

From over the edge of their forward rifle pit in the Carolina sand, the five *Iosco* sailors strained to see the beach. Beyond the drop-off near the water's edge, only the top half of the line of sailors streaming southward was visible. Blue jackets and blue round hats melded into a human river three-quarters of a mile from Fort Fisher's landface. Ships' flags and pennants waved aloft, led by fluttering Stars and Stripes.

More rebel soldiers crowded the fort's wall, rifles balanced over sandbags. From the river side of the fortress, rebels sprinted in twos and threes across the traverses toward the ocean, spilling into the Northeast Bastion. The gray line ringing the top of the bastion filled in.

The approaching sailors jounced their flags, as if they had already won the battle and were celebrating. They were sectioned into three distinct groups, one behind the other, mere yards apart. Near each ship's flag, officers carried raised swords.

Rebel marksmen fired toward the beach. A Union flag disappeared from view, only to immediately pop back up as another sailor thrust it aloft.

"They got almost a mile," Seamus said. Like Patrick, he switched his attention between the blue river and the gray fort.

"Less," Patrick said. "They can do it."

Directly in front of them, rebels reloaded the two twelve-pounder Napoleon field artillery pieces outside the fort's sally port. Within seconds, each cannon discharged a blast at the blue line. Shells of grape exploded near the front, ripping a gap in the column. The surrounding sailors picked up their pace, and the blue river stretched. The sailors to the rear quickened their own pace, and the line bunched up. The separation between the groups disappeared, and the force dissolved into one long, onrushing mass.

The sailors closed to within a thousand yards. Although rebel sharp-shooters maintained targeted fire, the other Confederates atop the wall patiently waited for the enemy to get closer.

"Them shooters, they aiming for the officers," Nat said as another Union flag disappeared before again springing back up.

Atop the wall, a cannon reverberated with a deep boom. Seconds later, a devastating blast ripped a wider gap in the front.

"A Columbiad," Seamus announced. "Our boats missed one."

"They'll get it," Patrick said.

"They can't with the boys going up that hill. They be too close," Nat said.

Another rebel cannon fired from the fort's seaface, hurling grape that exploded up the beach. The river kept coming.

Union gunboats fired almost simultaneously, and the *Iosco* sailors in the rifle pit watched as a plume of smoke and blue fire shot up from the fort's seaface. The rebel cannon did not fire again.

"Six hundred yards," Seamus announced.

The Napoleons from the sally port kept up their barrage, firing faster. Their gunners selected gaps in the terrain, targeting sections of beach to which they had a clear view. The Union sailors poured into the killing field.

"Four hundred," Seamus said.

At three hundred yards, the Columbiad scored another direct hit on the front of the line, spilling flags and raised swords in a swirl of dust and sand. The line paused, and sailors pushed into it from behind, creating a bulge to the land side. Then the river was flowing again, and above the sound of rebel gunfire and cannonading, Patrick heard the voices of the sailors emitting one long huzzah in their onward rush.

At two hundred yards, the sailors reached the palisade, and the line slowed as it squeezed past the narrow gap along the ocean.

"Where're the marines?" Seamus asked. "There's supposed to be four hundred of them."

Patrick scanned the beach. Some marines had dug in and were now directing cover fire at the fort, but no more than fifty or sixty of them. Toward the rear of the line, he saw the rest. They had abandoned their firing position and joined the plunging horde. They were now part of the blue river—running, stumbling, and screaming as it raced south, rifles raised impotently above their heads.

At one hundred seventy-five yards, a rebel officer climbed atop the parapet, sword pointing skyward. He barked a command. The line of gray atop the wall responded, moving in unison and pointing their rifles in a solid horizontal line at the onrushing sailors. At one hundred fifty yards, the officer deliberately lowered his sword directly at the blue mass and screamed. The line of gray exploded as one, gun smoke running the length of the fort's wall so thick that it shrouded the shooters.

Poured into the narrow width of the blue river, the Minié balls toppled rows of men. The Union column paused as sailors fell, blocking those behind. The line had just resumed moving when a second volley rang out, delivering similar death.

The Union line stopped again, and this time sailors dove to the side, seeking cover in the terrain. Some who had not yet reached the palisade circled to their right behind the fence's shattered timbers.

Other sailors renewed the charge, and the river again gurgled forward.

The rebels atop the wall were divided into two lines, shooters in front. After each volley, they passed their muskets to the line behind in exchange for loaded weapons.

A third volley exploded, and the blue line halted. The sailors began to scatter. Some dove to the ground and lay flat. Some dropped and began furiously digging with their knives and swords. Others turned and ran back up the beach, only to be shot down from behind with the fourth volley. More rebels raced to the bastion from the west, joining in the exuberance of the kill.

The rebels no longer fired in volleys. Each soldier aimed at selected targets. If a blue-clad body on the ground tried to crawl, geysers of sand kicked up around him until he lay still.

One Union officer stood and, grabbing a flag, exhorted his comrades to resume the charge. They were now only a hundred yards from the landface. Patrick heard him scream that if they climbed the sloping wall they would have the advantage. A few rose with him, but others got to their feet and raced north, back up the beach, stumbling headlong into those still plodding south.

As Patrick watched the rebel muskets pour death into the ranks, he knew that any chance of a renewed charge was gone.

The cheering from the beach had stopped, replaced instead by the euphoric shouts from atop the wall. Rebels stood on the sandbagged parapet, waving their muskets in one hand and jeering at the sailors. The only answer from the beach was the cries of the wounded and dying.

Seamus slumped against the inside of the rifle pit, his back to the beach.

Patrick crouched low, his head in his hands.

"Lordy, look," Nat said from the other end of the pit. "Good Lord, look," he repeated when no one responded.

Patrick slowly raised his head. Over at the river, the lead units of Curtis's brigade had started their own charge toward the rebel fort, regimental colors again held high.

CHAPTER 23

Fort Fisher

At the landface, in front of the main sally port

January 15, 1865

Midafternoon

The five *Iosco* sailors scrambled to the western edge of the rifle pit. A horde of Union soldiers ran down the Wilmington Road. In the lead was the tallest officer Patrick had ever seen, his hat perched atop the guidon he held high in his right hand.

At the wooden bridge, only the middle section of the line raced across the wooden planks. Men on either side waded through the marsh, rifles above their heads. At the palisade, an advance contingent hacked away with axes, widening the opening through which the soldiers squeezed.

Most of the rebels who had been atop the western end of the wall guarding the gate minutes earlier were gone, having dashed to the Northeast Bastion to repel the sailors. Only a smattering of gray troops remained, and as Newton Curtis's brigade bore down, they poured fire into the ranks while yelling back to their right. One hundred seventy-five yards from the fort, an entrenched line of Union sharpshooters furiously worked their repeating carbines, suppressing rebel fire.

Across the bridge and through the marsh, the column raced for another seventy-five yards until it veered left and spread out in a line parallel with the landface. Reaching the sloping walls, the federals bent forward and charged uphill at the westernmost rebel battery. They fired as they climbed and did not stop to reload. The rebel infantry returned a withering fire down the slope. Union soldiers dropped and tumbled back, sliding to the bottom.

Rebel cannon at the westernmost battery blew gaps in the Union column as it streamed across the bridge.

Still, the Union column advanced. When it reached the western gun emplacement, fighting devolved into hand-to-hand combat. The Union, with the advantage of numbers, quickly overwhelmed the artillerymen.

Other federals raced to the top of the first traverse, from where they directed fire down at rebel gun emplacements and infantry on the lower sections.

The rebels in the Northeast Bastion, triumphant from their defeat of the sailors, spotted the riverside advance. Patrick watched as they raced back up and down the wall to defend their western gate.

The artillery crew manning the Napoleons at the sally port swung their field pieces away from the beach, aiming instead toward the Wilmington Road. The cannons discharged shot and shell into the flanks of the Union charge.

"They're up the wall!" Landsman Vranken exclaimed. "They've got it!"

"Not yet," Seamus cautioned. "The rebs are coming back along the top."

"Cannon!" Nat yelled and pointed back at the road.

The gate at the western edge of the landface was piled with sandbags. As the sailors watched, three rebel soldiers rolled yet another twelve-pounder Napoleon out in front of the gate and aimed it into the face of the charging column. Off to its left at the river's edge, a rebel Parrot Rifle was hurriedly being readied.

The Napoleon at the gate fired seconds before the Parrot, and the twin explosions crumpled Union soldiers and destroyed much of the bridge. The federal charge continued.

Shots again buried into the sand behind them, and the five sailors ducked back down.

"We can't stay here," Phillips said. "Those rebs have spotted us."

"We can't go back neither," Patrick said as another round of bullets whizzed past.

The top of the wall was a swirl of clubbing and bayoneting. The two sides disengaged and retreated to the tops of the first and second traverses respectively. The rebel gun emplacement between the first two traverses lay dormant—the cannon knocked out, its crew sprawled dead around their gun.

As the rear of Curtis's brigade reached the bridge, a second Union brigade raced from the tree line and occupied the earthworks from which the first brigade had launched their charge.

Nat squinted at the blue-clad soldiers.

"That's Colonel Pennypacker's brigade," he said.

On a command the sailors could not hear, the second brigade rose up from the earthworks and began its own charge toward the fort.

Seamus faced his four shipmates. "We can go, or we can stay in this hole till hell freezes over," he said.

"We no come here to watch, boss," Nat said.

Patrick looked back to the ocean, where the bodies of his fellow sailors littered the sand. He saw John Barber, not forty feet from the pit. He looked at Vranken and Phillips, who looked at each other before nodding.

Patrick swallowed.

"We can use that broken fence to hide us," Seamus said. "We run along right behind it. We join that second brigade and get into the fort. We go where they go."

"I's ready," Nat Davis said, and his hand tightened around his cutlass.

Seamus studied the fire from the wall, raised his hand, and then yelled, "Now!"

Seamus was out first, followed by Nat and Patrick. As Patrick rolled over the edge and sprinted toward the stockade fence, he heard the two sailors running behind him.

Reaching the wall, Seamus ducked behind an undamaged section. When all five reached the fence, he sprinted out for the river.

Galusha Pennypacker's brigade had caught up with the tail end of Curtis's, just past the bridge. Instead of picking their way through the gaps in the palisade, Pennypacker's men swung wide, right around its end. Once past the palisade, the left side of Pennypacker's brigade followed Curtis's up the traverse, firing at the wall's defenders as they advanced. The right side headed straight at the gate and its rebel cannons.

Patrick outdistanced his compatriots and joined the mob flanking the fence. He veered right, directly toward the gate and the rebel cannon the Confederates were frantically reloading. He measured the distance. The artillerymen would not have enough time before he reached them.

The mass of blue screamed and hollered. There was no form to its attack. A desperate, tumbling, screeching mob raced for the gate.

Rebel rifles extended over the sandbags, puffs of smoke rising behind them. In the screaming melee of which he was now a part, Patrick could not hear firing. The sight of smoke from the muskets' discharge made him run faster and scream louder.

The mob rushed the cannon. When the rebels refused to surrender, they were cut down in a hail of bullets, while Union officers at the head of the column hacked at them with swords. The federal mob was now at the wall, soldiers firing over the stack of sandbags into the parade ground and putting their shoulders to the barricade. The soldier next to Patrick yanked the top sandbag off the wall. Patrick did the same, and soon the whole mob was tugging and yanking and spilling sandbags to the ground. The mob slithered through a breach—shooting, clubbing, and slashing.

Patrick jumped across, exhilarated. He was inside the fort. Some defenders threw up their hands. The Union fire continued, cutting down even those trying to surrender. The mist of gray retreated, and Union soldiers fired after it, cursing and swearing at the enemy as they ran.

"Form a line! Form a line!" an officer exhorted, but the mob ignored him, instead reloading and firing across the parade ground at anything that moved.

More Union soldiers pushed in from behind, and Patrick realized that, in the rush to the fort, he had neither unholstered his revolver nor drawn his sword. He now did both—sword in right hand, revolver in left—and joined the surge into the interior of the fort.

The push through the portal intensified, the mob bulging into a semicircle inside the gate.

Officers tried to regain control—screaming orders, grabbing soldiers, and raising hands. They tried organizing the soldiers into a defensive line and screeched instructions to everyone to get down and reload.

"They'll counterattack!" they yelled.

Patrick lay in the dirt, part of the advance semicircle. His heart raced. He sucked in deep breaths to calm himself. He held his revolver and his sword in front of him. When no countercharge materialized, he sat back and looked around. The parade ground was awash with shattered timbers and deep craters after three days of naval shelling. He was proud that his branch had done this, and hoped the soldiers around him understood and appreciated it.

The craters and debris provided cover for pockets of the enemy, who returned sporadic fire. The defenders were disorganized, and their return fire mostly passed harmlessly over the heads of the Union invaders. Trenching implements were brought up, and the federals began to dig pits.

Atop the parapet to his left, Patrick saw Union soldiers fighting traverse to traverse, possessed of the same animalistic abandon he had just experienced.

Deep booms echoed from the south, and rebel shells impacted around him. He recalled the isolated battery south of the fort, and knew that his fleet would target it. He dug faster with his own knife.

To his left, he spied Seamus. Patrick was about to call out to him when the soldier lying to his right tugged on his elbow.

"You're a sailor," the soldier said, more as a statement than a question.

When Patrick did not respond, the soldier continued. "We saw a bunch of you coming out of those pits as we started our charge."

"A bunch?" Patrick asked. He knew of only the five *Iosco* sailors.

The soldier considered. "Maybe fifteen, twenty, maybe more. A lot joined Curtis's brigade when they went in."

"What happened to them?" he asked.

The soldier nodded up the wall. "They're there now, fighting with the New Yorkers."

A rustling behind him made Patrick turn. A Union general entered the parade ground, surrounded by his staff.

"That's General Adelbert Ames," the soldier said. "He's the head of this regiment."

The general turned to a major standing by his side.

"Bring up Colonel Bell's brigade at once," he commanded, "and finish this."

CHAPTER 24

Fort Fisher

Inside the River Road sally port

January 15, 1865

Afternoon

The bodies of soldiers from both sides lay strewn about the disabled rebel gun emplacement in the riverside gate. Nat Davis moved among the Union fallen, pausing and kneeling at each. Some moaned and clutched at gaping wounds that leaked red onto their blue uniforms. Others lay in grotesque and fantastic positions and did not move. The wounded able to walk shuffled out the gate and back up the Wilmington Road to the field hospital above the tree line. Stretcher-bearers had not yet arrived to remove those who could not, and the graves detail would not bury the fallen until the battle was over. Until then, all the medics could do was identify which fallen soldiers would be moved back up the road and which would be stacked along the wall to await final disposition.

But Nat was not kneeling to help the fallen. He reached into the pockets and ammunition pouches of each Union soldier to retrieve as many rounds as he could scavenge for the musket he had picked off the ground and now held in his right hand.

If he was going to fight along the wall or into the fort, he would need more than a revolver. And fighting was something he was going to keep doing. Many of his shipmates on the *Iosco* had taunted him ever since he had enlisted. Of all that had been said, there was one accusation by Landsman Vranken that rang true—Nat Davis wanted to kill Southerners.

Unlike many of his fellow colored sailors and soldiers, Nat had escaped north with Jacob Joseph before the war, arriving in Bayonne, New Jersey, in the summer of 1857. Although Jacob settled in Brooklyn, obtaining a job on the docks, Nat continued north and found his way to Rochester.

Rochester was a central hub of the Underground Railroad, serving as the last port for runaway slaves smuggled by boat down the Genesee River and across Lake Ontario into Canada. Nat moved between the family farms of those secretly active in the Railroad, never staying anywhere too long and assisting other escapees as he could. Nat was taught to read and write in one of the county's underground reading rooms, operated by the local Methodist congregation.

The nation was on its slide to war. Despite his need to lay low, lest slave catchers locate him, Nat traveled all over upstate New York to listen to lectures and debates. After he learned to read, he spent countless evenings studying the topics of the day.

Nat knew the debates well. He also read speeches and writings by Southern politicians hoping to "explain their side of the issue."

But Nat knew that it was all a bunch of what he called "Southern Drivel." The politicians could speak passionately about the Southern way of life, the Southern culture, the desire for local governance, the importance of the document both sides claimed supported their position, called the Constitution. In the end, it was all a bunch of horse manure. There were only two reasons for this war: men in the South wanted to dissolve the Union, and they wanted to continue the "God-given" right to enslave other human beings.

Unlike his shipboard friend Seamus Flanagan—or his captain, John Guest, who spoke at Sunday services—Nat did not care about preserving the Union. He just cared about ending slavery. He could not imagine any god approving such a practice. In his mind, there was no way to justify it, and those who spoke about financial issues or culture or way of life were liars for whom the Lord had reserved a special place in hell.

They spoke well enough, Nat admitted. They fancied their words and tried to confuse the issues, but he knew. They believed that white men were superior to the Negro, so white men should rule. Everything else they said was a fog.

His great-grandfather had been enslaved and brought from Africa. And for the generations since, the culture had remained the same. The forefathers of his family's owners had used the term "states' rights" as justification to do what they wanted. He had no doubt that, when this war ended and the Negro was free, the descendants of those owners would still use that term to dominate others. The only way to stop it, to break this vicious cycle, as some abolitionists preached, was to render it asunder—to destroy every aspect of it, to kill every Southerner who supported it.

The abolitionists Nat heard in New York were sure of it. John Brown had been sure of it. Nat was as sure of this as he was of the lash, and he believed it with the finality of the auctioneer's gavel.

Up the road, Louis Bell's brigade double-timed toward the fort through a hail of shot and shell. Nat hurriedly gathered up the powder and bullets from the soldier over whose body he knelt and unbuckled the fallen soldier's pouch. Standing, he rebuckled it onto himself and dropped in the rounds.

The rebels on the ramparts fired down the wall, slicing into Colonel Bell's advancing brigade. He feared they had regained a section of the landface. As Bell's column approached the remnants of the bridge, the lead officer in a colonel's uniform dropped, clutching his chest. The soldiers who stopped to assist him also quickly fell.

Still, the column continued, balancing across the exposed joists of the damaged bridge and wedging through the palisade. When the Union soldiers reached the gate, Nat turned with them and raced up the slope, his newly acquired musket held firmly.

Curtis's brigade, supported by part of Pennypacker's, was battling traverse by traverse. Nat raced up one and then down, past the first rebel gun emplacement, and then back up again, until he reached the front battle line.

Union soldiers crouched behind the crest of a traverse, firing across at the next one. After each soldier fired, he slid down to reload. Another Union soldier quickly scampered up and took his place. The enemy fire slackened, and Nat thought that the rebels were being beaten back. A Union officer screamed "Charge!" and federals stood and raced down the traverse and up the next, screaming the whole way.

At the top of the next traverse, the hand-to-hand fighting resumed as Union soldiers clubbed and stabbed throughout their steady advance.

Even along the narrow parapet, the Union's superior numbers were turning the battle's outcome.

Nat sat to reload as the advancing wave passed him. He yanked a cartridge from his pouch. From farther along the wall came a growing rebel yell. Rising to his knees, Nat peered over the mound. Racing toward him was a rebel officer in a general's uniform, sword raised, leading a counterattack out of the Northeast Bastion. Nat raised his musket and fired, as did several other Union soldiers around him. The lead rebels, including the general, collapsed in a heap.

Another Union charge was ordered, and his fellow soldiers again plunged headlong toward their enemies.

CHAPTER 25

Federal Point, North Carolina
27th United States Colored Regiment
January 15, 1865

Private Jim Jeffereds leaned over the breastworks and stared across the open terrain. The 27th had dug their fortifications in the early morning hours Saturday, and the regiment had been hunkered behind them since. Two hundred yards in front of him was a line of Union skirmishers, and seventy yards farther, five pickets hid just inside the stand of pine. An enemy attacking down the peninsula would draw fire from the pickets, who would retreat to the skirmish line. The gunfire would alert the skirmishers and the soldiers behind the breastworks, giving both time to prepare a defensive fire line. The Union skirmishers would then retreat to the protection of the reinforced trench.

Behind him, Jim heard gunfire from the fort. The naval bombardment of the landface was over, and only the seaface was now targeted by the gunboats.

Reserves would soon be needed at the fort. His unit might yet march south. But until so ordered, their job was to keep any Confederates from attacking the Union rear. So far, the pickets had seen no movement in the woods.

"We get any messengers?" William Carney asked.

Jim Jeffereds turned away and slumped to the ground, his back against the breastworks.

"Nothing," he said. "I think they'll only send a runner if they need us down there."

Pulling the stopper off his canteen, he took several gulps.

"Of course," Jim continued, wiping his mouth with his sleeve, "they can't use us unless they get someone else to guard their arse. And there ain't no one else."

At the sound of two musket shots from the east, Jim swiveled to his left. Other men along the line turned. More shots rang out, staccato-like.

"Them's Abbott's men," William Carney said, "over by the ocean."

Jim grabbed his musket and stood. He tried to look east, but his view was blocked by pine. He turned north, surveying the open terrain. His fellow soldiers on the skirmish line also looked back toward the Atlantic. Another series of shots echoed from the east.

"The pickets, they got something," Carney said.

Captain Pinney raced along the line, gripping the hilt of his sheathed sword with his left hand. When he got to Jim, he stopped and pointed.

"Ephraim Perkins!" he yelled, calling the unit's drummer boy, who sat cross-legged behind the barricade. The fourteen-year-old jumped to his feet and raced to the captain, who was already writing. Captain Pinney rolled the note and handed it to the boy.

"Take this to Colonel Abbott's command at the beach. Find him or any officer. Find out what's happening. Now listen carefully," he said, grabbing the youth roughly by the shoulders. "I need to know if Abbott is under attack and if they can hold. Do you understand?"

The youth nodded vigorously.

"Our lives depend on this," the captain continued. "If they're getting overrun, get back here as fast as you can. Even without a return dispatch. Now go, and run like the devil himself was after you."

The lad ran off. The captain turned back to the line.

"If Abbott is overrun, they'll try to flank us," William said to Jim.

"Shall we form a line to the right?" the tall soldier with the deep voice asked the officer.

The captain did not answer. He called over a lieutenant, and together they prowled the line, dividing the soldiers into two groups by designating every other man.

"If they attack from the north, Line One will form a direct line," the captain said. "You men in the second line, stay back in reserve and take the front upon command.

"If they get around Abbott, I want Line Two to form at a right angle, straight back."

Off toward the river, other officers in the 27th moved up and down behind the barricade, speaking with their companies. To the rear, soldiers stacked ammunition crates closer to the trench. The men of the 27th stood relaxed at the barricade and waited. Several chewed tobacco.

Ephraim Perkins returned at a run. The soldiers turned to the boy, but he sprinted right to Captain Pinney.

"Abbott's men holding, sir," he huffed. He paused long enough to suck in a deep breath. "The skirmishers were overrun, but the line held, and the rebs pulled back."

"I told you them New Hampshire white boys could hold Hoke," William said proudly. He looked around, smiling and nodding, as if expecting his fellow soldiers to acknowledge his military expertise.

Gunfire erupted from the trees. Jim pushed up against the barricade. Several soldiers pointed their muskets northward. Union pickets sprinted from the tree line, diving into the pits of the skirmishers.

"Looks like them rebs be trying to come this way," William said, swinging his own musket over the wall of logs.

Jim peered down the barrel of his Springfield and tried to acquire a target in the woods. He saw nothing.

Soldiers in the forward rifle pit gestured wildly at the trees. A volley rang out from the woods, flashing sparks of yellow and red, but the gun smoke from the rebel firing was obscured by the shadows.

The Union skirmisher line leveled its own controlled volley into the woods and then, at the command of a sergeant, jumped up and retreated to the barricade, tumbling around Jim. They scrambled to their feet and reloaded.

Captain Pinney screamed orders. Everyone moved tight to the barricade. With the skirmishers now behind them, the 27th had an open field of fire.

"How many?" the captain demanded.

"Woods are full," one of the pickets answered as he rammed a Minié ball down the barrel of his musket. He removed the ramrod and studied his weapon, carefully checking the hammer.

"At least two companies, maybe more to the left," he continued. "They look to be bringing up more through them trees."

Captain Pinney yanked paper from his belt pouch. "Perkins!" he yelled, even as he scribbled. When the drummer boy reappeared, the captain shoved the dispatch at him.

"Get this to the beach. Give it to the signal corps. The boats know our position. We need fire one hundred fifty yards in front of us, all the way into the woods."

Grabbing the dispatch wordlessly this time, the boy turned and ran back toward the ocean.

A lieutenant moved along the line, reminding the soldiers of the two groups. Line One would fire first and move back, while Line Two took its place. They should only fire upon command. He kept repeating the two orders, over and over.

"This is it," William Carney said. "This is it."

Jim nodded. "If we don't hold them here, the whole army goes to hell."

"I guess it all comes down to this," William said. "The whole damn war. Lordy, don't it?"

"They're getting ready, men!" the captain announced. "Line One. Ready."

There was motion in the woods. Jim snugged tighter to the barricade, while the men from Line Two stepped back. He still couldn't see a target.

"Hold your fire until the command," the lieutenant cautioned.

From the woods, a fierce yell erupted, and a gray mass rushed out, regimental and battle flags aloft in the middle. Several Union soldiers fired.

"Not yet, damn it, not yet!" the lieutenant shouted. He raced to the soldiers who fired, pulling them roughly off the line with a command to reload and then grabbed and shoved replacements from Line Two to the barricade.

The rebels kept coming, their cry rising in volume as they rushed headlong toward the company.

"They're going to take those rifle pits," Jim said.

Captain Pinney moved between Jim and William and nodded. He placed a hand on Jim's shoulder.

"You could be right, Carney," he said, without turning to look at the soldier. "This could be it, the whole damn war right here."

Jim wanted to fire. He wanted to let loose at the bastard horde that bore down, to rip into flesh with ball and bayonet, to kill every overseer and owner who ever lived. His heart raced, and he felt what the soldiers called "battle energy," when he believed he could rush anywhere at any speed and do anything. Six months earlier, he would have let loose, firing like the new soldiers had down the line. But he had learned to wait.

"Ready, men," the captain repeated calmly. "Ready . . ."

The men extended their muskets as one, a solid row of Springfields pointing north.

The gray line veered, angling to Jim's right. *They want to flank us,* he thought. He could hear rebel officers screaming commands and tried to identify where they were. He wanted an officer.

"Ready . . . ready . . ."

He still couldn't discern individual faces. Maybe that was better.

"Ready . . . Now! Fire!"

The Union line exploded in an avalanche of shot, hurled at the onrushing gray mass. Not finding an officer, Jim targeted the standard-bearer and watched him collapse from his shot, his regimental flag pitching forward.

The federal volley was devastating. Rebels fell in twisted piles. The horde hesitated but then resumed, angling even more to Jim's right.

"Line One, back!" the captain screamed. "Reload. Line Two, forward!"

Jim moved back, dropping the stock of his musket to the ground in one motion. Holding his rifle with his left hand, he reached into his ammunition pouch with his right and yanked out a paper cartridge holding both a measured amount of gunpowder and a .58 caliber Minié ball. Ripping the top with his teeth, he poured the measured powder and ball into the barrel, crumpled the paper, and shoved it in on top. He removed the ramrod from the sling beneath the barrel and rammed the powder, ball, and paper home. The crumpled paper forced the powder to the rear of the bore. Lifting the musket, he placed a percussion cap on the hammer. Holding his Springfield at eye level, he searched for his second target.

He noticed how calmly he worked and was pleased that, next to him, William was also efficient. Some soldiers' hands were shaking, and one dropped his ramrod. At Camp Delaware, his sergeant had insisted that every soldier be able to load and shoot six rounds in two minutes, but in battle, trembling hands reduced speed.

Captain Pinney appeared to be stalling to give Line One time to reload. He kept barking commands to remain steady, but his own voice was rising. Battle energy.

"Ready . . . Ready . . . Now! Kill the bastards!" the captain screamed. "No-good, traitorous, lying bastards! Shoot their balls off. Kill every one!" the captain screamed again, his pitch rising higher with each oath. "They're a bunch of traitorous, slimy, bitch-fucking, Mary bastards who don't deserve to live. Kill them! Kill every fucking one of them and send their dratted kind to the blazes itself!"

Jim only heard half the oaths, as the firing from Line Two was more selective than the unified killing volley of Line One. But the death was the same.

Jim was back at the line with loaded musket. The horde slowed, and Jim saw more rebels drop to the ground than were being shot. They were losing their nerve. Up and down the line, the 27th poured musketry into the gray line, and the line wavered.

Other officers exclaimed similar exhortations, as if they personally knew each soldier rushing headlong toward them and hated each one. Jim fired again and watched another rebel fall.

Several rebels reached the rifle pits. The Union order came to stop firing, the lieutenants yelling the command up and down the line. The gray attack was broken, and though formidable numbers lay scattered in the field in front of the Union line, the rebel strength as an attacking force was gone.

Jim heard the loud, deep, arcing whoosh of a large projectile, and the field in front of him convulsed. A row of dirt geysers shot skyward, and then the sequence of eruptions steadily drifted back until the pines themselves toppled, thick trees severed like saplings. The rebels still alive in front of him leapt to their feet and raced back for the trees before swinging left, tumbling into the section of woods not under bombardment. More ships offshore joined the barrage, and Jim watched as rebels threw down their weapons and raced in every direction behind the tree line. Whatever brigade had charged at him was now on the run. It would take a day for the enemy to find their surviving soldiers and sort them to their units. He lowered his musket, resting its stock on the ground.

Captain Pinney stood behind him, red-faced and panting.

"Lord," William said slowly, studying his captain. "If you go to church, Captain, you better say a prayer to the baby Jesus, thanking him that you weren't born a slave."

Still panting, the captain stared, confused, at the private.

"What?" he asked.

"'Cause after all that cussin' you just done, Captain, iffin' you was, they'd call you one crazy nigger."

CHAPTER 26

Fort Fisher

January 15, 1865

Late afternoon

Lieutenant Pinson knew the fort was in trouble. Union forces had reached the riverside gate and were working their way along the traverses, forcing the Confederates back toward the Northeast Bastion. The Union's second wave had gotten through the gate and set up a defensive line within the fort. General Whiting had led a strike against the intruders advancing along the parapets. The counterattack had failed, and the general now lay wounded in the fort's hospital room in the bombproof beneath Pulpit Battery.

Union Navy shells pounded the landface and, with each thud, the lamplights flickered. Stretcher-bearers trotted into the hospital room, lifting one end or the other of their wounded cargo to negotiate the twists of the cramped quarters. Doctors checked each soldier before directing the bearers to one of three areas. Along the back wall, bodies were stacked up roughly, a blood-soaked sheet thrown over the pile.

Colonel Lamb had not given up. He stood over the general's cot, the pair plotting strategy.

"I tried," General Whiting said between labored breaths. "They're dug in a semicircle, protecting the river gate. We can't stop them from running up the walls and reinforcing their attack along the traverses if we can't get through that gate. They've got a whole trench and just keep adding men. Now they're wheeling cannon into the fort."

"General Bragg," Colonel Lamb said. "He has to attack now, or all is lost."

Turning and spotting Lieutenant Pinson, the colonel motioned him over.

"We need to send a telegram to General Bragg," the colonel said. "Send a runner to Battery Buchanan to signal across the river."

Lieutenant Pinson pulled paper from his belt.

"We still hold the fort but are sorely pressed," General Whiting dictated. "Can't you assist us from the outside?"

When he finished scribbling, Lieutenant Pinson searched for an able-bodied messenger.

Caleb Cuthbait ducked through a doorway and entered, a bandage wrapped around his left arm. The lieutenant rejected sending him to the battery. He might need the sergeant later.

"How bad?" the lieutenant asked Caleb when the sergeant approached.

"I was fortunate," Caleb answered. "We were trying to cover the beach, and a shell hit our powder. I only got a bruise."

"The crew?" Lieutenant Pinson asked.

"Corporal Jennings is dead. Wainwright. The young boy from Roanoke. Pelletier is wounded badly. He's somewhere here," Caleb said, searching among the cots.

The lieutenant nodded. Spotting a stretcher-bearer heading out the doorway, he grabbed the medic and handed him the written note, instructing him to leave immediately for Battery Buchanan.

"The seaface?" the lieutenant asked, but Caleb just shook his head.

"Another message for the general?" Caleb asked, nodding toward the departing stretcher-bearer.

"The general and colonel still think that General Bragg will come down."

"And if he doesn't?" Caleb asked.

The lieutenant described the state of the fort. "They're pouring reinforcements up the traverses. They hold the gate. We don't have enough men on the wall to lay sustained fire on their reinforcing columns."

"We need another counterattack," Colonel Lamb said. When Caleb and the lieutenant stared at him blankly, he explained.

"We need to retake the river gate. If we can get through, turn the cannons back on the road, maybe slow the reinforcements, the men on the wall can hold until Bragg arrives."

General Whiting rose up on one arm from his cot. "That's possible," he said.

"We don't have the men," the lieutenant countered. "We're still trying to hold the yard, and we can't spare anyone off the wall. And if the Yankees get the wall, they'll shoot down into the whole yard."

The colonel surveyed the dimly lit hospital room.

"From here, then," he announced. "Round up every man who can walk—the wounded, stretcher-bearers, medics, everyone. We organize one charge for the gate, get through to the other side, and charge the Wilmington Road to cut them off. We might be able to hold the fort until . . ."

He didn't finish his thought.

"The gate, yes," the lieutenant said, "but with wounded?" He gestured around the room. "These men have been through a lot already, Colonel. Attacking across the yard is crazy. I've seen how dug in the Yankees are. Reaching the gate is near impossible."

The lieutenant stopped when he saw the colonel glaring at him.

Lieutenant Pinson nodded. "I'll see to it, sir."

Caleb and the lieutenant circled the hospital room, soliciting volunteers. Many were bandaged but could still walk. Within minutes, they assembled forty walking wounded and stretcher-bearers. Leaving them in the hospital room, they went off to search the bombproofs, collecting muskets.

When they returned, the lieutenant approached Colonel Lamb again.

"Sir, when we come out of the bombproofs, we'll be in direct fire from the Yankee circle. The men we have left on the parade ground can't suppress their fire."

"I know," the colonel said. "Sergeant!" the colonel commanded, calling to Caleb. "There is one Napoleon just outside. Can you and the lieutenant get it loaded?"

Caleb nodded.

"Very well," the colonel continued. "When we come out, lay down a charge of grape at the Union bulge. It should be enough to make them take cover and allow us to reach them."

Colonel Lamb turned to the assembled group. Every soldier appeared bandaged.

"Once our cannon fires, we dash for the gate. Fight our way through it and retake the cannons. Lay fire on the road and charge behind it. We dig in and hold until General Hoke attacks the federals from the rear. Are you ready?"

When the men gave a rousing huzzah, the colonel turned to Pinson. "Whenever you're ready, Lieutenant."

Caleb and the lieutenant ducked out the doorway and crouch-walked to the idle Napoleon in the yard. Broken bodies littered the earth. Those still alive but unable to move cried out. The remaining Confederates were clumped across the yard in disorganized groups. The Union forces continued to target stragglers, and the Confederate's return fire was waning.

Caleb and Daniel spun and loaded the cannon.

"You realize this is a suicide charge," the lieutenant grunted as they rammed the grape shell down the barrel. "Probably four thousand on the wall and in the yard."

"We have no choice," Caleb answered as he lifted the carriage's tongue and swung the gun. When it was pointed toward the Union line, Lieutenant Pinson turned and called back to the bombproof. Immediately, Colonel Lamb led a charge out from the bombproof behind the cannon. The Confederate line angled across the parade ground toward the riverside gate.

For a brief moment, Lieutenant Pinson envisioned the charge succeeding. In his mind, he saw the gray line, trimmed with white and oozing red, fighting its way through the gate and retaking the Wilmington Road.

But, on command, the left side of the Union entrenchment rose up as one and fired. The blue line leaped over their earthen fortification and charged back at the advancing Confederates. A Union sailor waving a naval cutlass led the countercharge. The lieutenant touched the botefeux to the touch hole. The countercharge evaporated in a cloud of debris and flying dirt and body parts. Almost immediately, the middle section of the Union line rose up and leveled a second volley into the charging Confederates.

Colonel Lamb pitched forward into the dirt. Seeing their leader fall, the soldiers behind him wavered, and the charge halted. Some bent to help those who had fallen. When a third section of the blue line fired another volley into the Confederate ranks, the charge collapsed. The soldiers turned and raced back to the bombproof.

Grabbing Caleb, Lieutenant Pinson tugged him back inside as well.

Doctors were already working on Colonel Lamb and the others. The colonel lay next to General Whiting.

Lieutenant Pinson pushed Caleb through the hospital room and down the connecting corridor.

"Where are we going?" Caleb demanded.

"Battery Buchanan," was the terse reply.

Caleb pulled away and faced his superior. "But our station is here," he protested.

"Look," the lieutenant replied. He pointed back toward the parade ground. "That was madness. There are not enough men in this fort to stop the Yankee attack. They're on the walls, in the fort, on the parade ground. They're bringing cannons up, and we have none left. They have eight to ten thousand out there in the woods, and we have less than a thousand left here. General Hoke has a division above them on the peninsula. Unless we can get Bragg to order him to attack . . ."

He broke off and resumed pushing Caleb down the tunnel.

"He's not understanding the situation," Pinson hissed. "The telegrams are not working. He does not believe our plight. We need to tell him and make him see, consequences be damned."

"I don't understand . . ." Caleb began, gesturing back toward the hospital room.

Private Peydreau entered the tunnel. Lieutenant Pinson grabbed the private by the arm and pinned him against the wall alongside his sergeant.

"Listen, you two," Pinson spat, "we need to get word to General Bragg, what is really going on here. Personal, not with a telegram."

"We're leaving?" Caleb asked incredulously. "That's desertion. That's—"

"We're not deserting anything," Pinson interrupted. "I need you two to get around the Yankee line."

He turned to the private. "There are boats at Battery Buchanan. Grab one—rowboat, launch, anything. Row upriver. Get to Sugar Loaf. Demand to see General Bragg. Don't take no from anyone. Tell him what's really going on. And you, Caleb," the lieutenant said, turning to the sergeant.

"You like to run. This is your chance. Circle around the fort by the seaface. Get on the Wilmington Road to Sugar Loaf. Tell the general what is happening and how desperate we are.

"And men," Pinson added, softening his tone, "I don't need to tell you what's at stake. This fort has maybe two or three more hours, no matter how many suicide attacks are ordered by madmen. Once it falls, the Yankees will reinforce it in the morning, and their fleet will destroy any counterassault by Hoke. If General Bragg does not send Hoke tonight, before the Yankees dig in, we're lost. And we know what that means."

Reaching out with his hands, he took both soldiers by their shoulders.

"Go," he said simply before turning and heading back to the hospital room.

When the lieutenant reentered the room, Colonel Lamb was speaking with Major Reilly, turning command of the fort over to him. Together with the general, they were planning another counterattack out of the bombproofs. Using Hagood's South Carolinians, who had arrived that day, Major Reilly estimated that he'd have about one hundred fifty soldiers with which to launch his assault. When the three finished their planning, they called over Lieutenant Pinson and asked him to prepare for the counterattack.

"Very good," the lieutenant answered and saluted.

CHAPTER 27

Fort Fisher
On the landface
January 15, 1865
Late afternoon

Colonel Newton Curtis stood atop the third traverse and, for the second time since landing, calculated how fortunate he was. The sailor attack down the beach, although a tactical disaster, had drawn rebel defenders away from the western wall to their Northeast Bastion, leaving the western end of the fort open. Curtis's brigade had gained a lightly challenged foothold. Pennypacker's reinforcements had overwhelmed the gate defenders, and Union forces now lay entrenched on the parade ground. The secured gate prevented any direct rebel counterassault on the Wilmington Road, keeping it open for reinforcements.

But despite the numerical superiority of the federal forces, progress along the landface was going slower than he had expected. Although, in the initial charge, Curtis's brigade had captured four of the fifteen traverses, Confederate counterattacks had slowed the advance, and fighting had dissolved into a hill-by-hill war of attrition.

Along the narrow parapet, Curtis's men were unable to take full advantage of their numerical superiority, now aided with the addition of Pennypacker's and Lewis Bell's brigades. Pennypacker had been seriously wounded and was not expected to recover, and Lewis Bell had been shot down before he reached the bridge. Newton Curtis was the sole remaining commanding officer of the three brigades that bunched together behind him.

Union soldiers crawled to the top of each traverse and fired over the top at Confederates who did the same. Once soldiers on both sides had discharged their single musket shot, the fighting for each traverse dissolved into a vicious struggle of wielded musket butt and bayonet thrust. The life expectancy of soldiers reaching the top of a traverse could be measured in minutes, and bodies from both sides piled so high on the slopes that soldiers behind them had trouble scrambling over the blood-soaked remains of their comrades.

Curtis knew that the Union would win this battle with time, but only because he had more lives to sacrifice than did the defenders.

The cost was rising. In addition to his two fellow brigade commanders, Colonel Moore was dead, Captain Thomas of the 117th New York had been killed on the third traverse, and that unit's Lieutenant Meyer was wounded.

In an effort to break the stalemate, Curtis personally led a bayonet charge from the third traverse, and the federals pushed the rebels back to the fourth, where fighting again bogged down. Soldiers from both sides again crawled to the top to shoot into the face of the enemy before the other did the same. The soldier who could swing the muzzle of his musket over the crest of the sand hill first had a temporary advantage, one that dissipated once he pulled the trigger.

The Union pushed the rebels over the fourth traverse and back to the fifth.

Sailors, who had dug forward rifle pits when the beach attack launched prematurely, had joined the soldier attack in the west and now fought hand-to-hand along the traverses with revolvers and cutlasses. Spotting a blue-jacketed Jack Tar, Curtis called him over. The sailor identified himself as Acting Master's Mate Silas Kempton of the *Santiago de Cuba*.

"Go back up the beach," the colonel commanded. "Find General Terry. Have the Signal Corps flag the fleet to lay down cannon fire atop this wall. Have them start at the eastern end and work westward to the fifth traverse, carefully and slowly. Do you understand?"

When the sailor acknowledged his assent, the colonel continued. "Make sure that the bombardment moves along the wall thoroughly. We need to clear the enemy off this wall."

Within half an hour, the naval fleet opened up on the wall, their fire slowly sweeping westward toward the fifth traverse. Some shells strayed too far, wreaking devastation on the front of the advancing Union line.

Despite the bombardment, more Confederates charged into the maelstrom. Union forces changed their tactics. Instead of crawling up each traverse and rising up to shoot into the faces of the soldiers on the other side, they began to merely reach over the top with their muskets and fire blindly down the other slope, sometimes getting shot in the hand in the process.

The Union gained the fifth traverse and then the sixth. As they approached the middle of the landface, above the rebel sally port, rebel artillerymen darted from the sally port to fire the two Napoleons at the troops streaming down the Wilmington Road.

In the parade ground to Curtis's right, the rebels mounted yet another counterattack from behind their earthworks. A major led the charge of a force Curtis estimated to be approximately one hundred fifty. The colonel was amazed at the audacity and courage of the enemy as they charged against a larger, dug in Yankee force on the parade ground. Over a hundred of the rebels were cut down before the rest retreated behind their earthworks.

On the parade ground, the two sides continued to exchange fire from behind their barriers. The Union soldiers, who were dug into their semicircle inside the gate, outnumbered the defenders behind their earthworks, and the rebel fire slowly tapered off.

They're running out of ammunition, Curtis thought with grim satisfaction.

Colonel Lyman led a Union advance along the inside of the landface wall until it reached opposite Curtis's own forward position atop the parapet. Lyman's men charged up the wall, flanking the defenders and capturing yet another traverse. But Newton Curtis watched in horror as Colonel Lyman was gunned down. With the capture of each traverse, the ground along the bottom of both sides of the wall was rendered secure for Union advances.

Curtis's men reached the seventh traverse above the sally port at the same time that a Union detachment under Lieutenant Ketcham, advancing along the outside of the fort, arrived. When Ketcham's squad fired into the mouth of the tunnel, the rebel artillerymen inside surrendered.

The rebels now had just the one lone Columbiad on the landface that was still firing up the road. Standing atop the seventh traverse, Curtis watched the rebels reloading. He assigned sharpshooters to pick off its crew, and the behemoth soon fell silent.

A veteran of the Peninsula Campaign, the Bermuda Hundred Campaign, and the Siege of Petersburg, Newton Martin Curtis knew the feel of victory, and he sensed it now. His men held half the wall, they had eliminated the enemy artillery, and his forces held a numerical superiority on the parade ground.

It was time to end the battle for the fort. The Union sailors' attempt to capture the Northeast Bastion had failed, but the strategy had been sound. If his men advanced the length of the wall along the ground in front of the landface, they could take the Bastion and attack the remaining wall defenders from the rear. Once surrounded, the rebels' only choice would be to abandon the landface and flee south across the open plain. The rout would be on.

Curtis dispatched a messenger to bring up more reinforcements. He would position them for an advance, which he would lead himself, along the outside of the wall. In minutes, the messenger returned, telling Curtis that his division commander, General Ames, now inside the gate on the parade ground, would not approve any more troops for the day. Curtis was ordered to entrench where he stood and resume the battle in the morning. The general would see to it that digging implements were sent forward.

Curtis spun around. The winter sun was setting behind the river, but there was still daylight. He had been pulled back from his objective three weeks earlier. He would not be deterred again.

"Go back to the general," he told the messenger. "Tell him we can finish this tonight. Have him send three companies along the front of the wall. I will lead them myself."

After the messenger departed, Curtis resumed directing the Union attack to capture the next traverse.

The aide was back in minutes.

"Sir, the general states that the men are exhausted, the units are all intermingled now, and over half his officers are dead. He orders you to dig in and reorganize for an attack in the morning. Spades are on their way up."

"Goddamn the general!" Curtis exclaimed.

The messenger stared, wide-eyed, at his blasphemous colonel.

"Go back again," Colonel Curtis said. "To hell with the general. Find some junior officers and tell them they are ordered to report to me with their commands."

Sputtering, the messenger again turned around. When he returned the third time, he carried an armful of spades.

"Sir, the general refuses your request and orders you to dig in where you stand. You are to use these."

Curtis flew at the messenger and wrenched the shovels from his arms.

"Use these?" the colonel screamed into the young soldier's face. "I'll show you how to use these."

Carrying them to the top of the traverse, where the battle raged, he drew himself up to his full height of six feet five inches and heaved the shovels over the crest at the enemy on the other side.

"Hey, Johnny!" he yelled above the roar of the battle. "You better dig and dig well, 'cause I'm coming for ya, and I'm coming tonight!"

Curtis turned and shoved the messenger aside. He spotted Acting Master's Mate Kempton, back after delivering the earlier message to General Terry requesting the fleet to rake the wall.

"Take another message," he commanded. "Find General Terry. Tell him we can take the fort tonight with a bold push, but I need more men to win final victory."

Kempton ran off.

Spotting Captain Magill of the 117th New York, Curtis instructed him to continue the fight along the wall. When Magill moved off, Curtis turned and strode back to the riverside gate.

He found the general consulting with Colonel Cyrus Comstock near the gate, a diagram of the fort in his hands.

"I've told you three times to entrench," the general said as Colonel Curtis approached. "The men are exhausted, there are no more cohesive units, just mobs milling about, and precious few officers left to lead. In the morning, we will resume the attack. We'll use reinforcements from Abbott's men to move along outside the wall and flank the enemy."

Colonel Curtis leaned in so that no one, save Cyrus Comstock, could hear.

"You're a damn fool, Ames," he spat. "I never should have listened to Butler last month, and I will not listen to you now. We need to win this war, and to do that, we need to capture this fort. The enemy is close to breaking. Their cannon is gone, they are almost off the wall, and those on the ground are running out of ammunition and have slackened their fire. Some are already retreating down the peninsula. If you are so pigheaded as to wait until tomorrow, they could reinforce this fort by the river and yet hold it. And if you pull either Abbott or Paine's coloreds off our northern defense, Hoke could sweep us out to sea."

General Ames stood stock-still, not saying a word, as Colonel Curtis finished his tirade. Comstock said nothing.

Colonel Curtis wheeled and began searching the area for volunteer officers to assist him in finishing the fight. Finding several, he left them to organize their men while he returned to the front.

Captain Magill had captured two more traverses, and the federals now fought for the tenth. Curtis was convinced, more than ever, that the rebels were done. He strode to the top of the ninth traverse and peered over. An explosion detonated above him, knocking him back and tumbling him down the slope. He landed at the bottom of the hill and did not move. Soldiers rushed to him. The left side of his face was blown away, and his left eye was gone. Not sure if he was alive, his soldiers lifted him onto a blanket and bore him out of the fort to the field hospital back up the road.

CHAPTER 28

Federal Point, North Carolina
27th United States Colored Regiment
January 15, 1865

Rumors flew up and down the line in the trench behind the earthworks that formed the Union's northern defense line. The units attacking the fort to their rear had been routed, and rebels were chasing the federals north. The enemy had surrendered, and the fight was over. Each rumor had its own supporters, who vigorously defended their position.

Remnants of messages from the runners dispatched in both directions—east to General Terry and south to the fort—fueled all rumors.

Jim Jeffereds didn't believe any of them. Ephraim Perkins, the fourteen-year-old musician, was being run ragged carrying messages back and forth to the ocean. Upon each return, Jim grabbed the youth to wring more details as to what was happening.

"General Ames," the boy huffed on his last return, "he wanted to entrench for the night. All his officers, all three of his brigade commanders, be down—Curtis, Pennypacker, and Bell. He done ask Colonel Comstock what to do. Colonel Comstock, he be friends with Ulysses Grant himself. Well, Colonel Comstock say that Colonel Curtis, he want to finish it tonight before he got wounded bad, so that's what they should do. And General Ames, he no want to upset General Grant, so now he agree with Colonel Curtis. Colonel Comstock say to the blazes with Hoke. Bring Abbott's men down, and let Hoke attack. We'll take the fort. And he want to use us coloreds too, so y'all better be ready to march, and I gots to get ready to drum."

Ephraim Perkins ran off to the beach with another message for General Terry.

"Can't be," the deep-voiced soldier said when told what the lad claimed. "General Terry is scared of Hoke. He won't pull Abbott's men off and leave our right wide open."

"It won't be no open," the tall soldier said. "I heard from Sammy Whittle that General Terry, why he gonna take all them sailors beaten up on the beach and make them stand for Abbott's men."

Several soldiers scoffed.

"How can a bunch of sailors take the place of Abbott's men?" they asked. "Them sailors gonna fight Hoke with navy swords and revolvers?"

A general guffaw ensued.

"We going too," Jim Jeffereds announced. "I heard it from little Ephraim himself."

"Not all of us," Captain Pinney boomed as he walked along the trench back toward his company. "You heard right about Colonel Comstock wanting all of General Paine's regiment, but it's not going to happen. General Terry did send Colonel Abbott and his brigade south to the fort and replaced them with sailors. The sailors are already in their place, and Colonel Abbott is heading down the beach even now. He's to cross the peninsula and enter the fort by the river. General Terry wants to keep most of General Paine's division here to guard the northern line, but he specifically asked—listen close, men—that General Paine's very best regiment be sent in to the fort, and that, men, means us, the 27th. So, grab your gear. We are moving out!"

"Lordy!" William Carney exclaimed, beaming again. "Did you hear that, Jim? I told you us coloreds were gonna take the fort and end this war."

"It's getting dark," Jim said, scanning the river and the sky above.

"But we got the moon," William said. "We can march in the moon. We did two nights ago to get here, and we can do it again."

Men gathered their gear, and Captain Pinney formed them up for their trek south. They would soon learn for themselves whether the Union was on the verge of victory or defeat. Jim hefted his pack. Within minutes, the 27th was heading down the Wilmington Road.

Three hundred yards north of where Captain Pinney hurriedly organized his company into formation, Seth Colburn lay in the woods and watched.

"Look at them niggers," he spat. "They making like a bunch of chickens and quitting rather than fightin' us."

"I dunno," Robert Dearborn mused next to him. "Them fought good when we done attack."

Seth scoffed. "They was scared and about to break when their goddam navy saved them."

"Seems to me," Robert drawled, "we was the ones a-breaking."

The pair watched the 27th disengage from behind their earthworks and move off south, leaving a temporary gap in the Union line in front of them.

"This our chance," Robert said. "Before their line fills in. We can go find our company now. That is, depending on how far they run," he chuckled. He crawled backwards several feet and began to stand.

"Don't be stupid!" Seth barked without moving. "We'll do no such thing. The penalty for being a spy is death by hanging, and now we's got our chance to execute the yellow-bellied Yankee spy that got Asa King dead."

CHAPTER 29

Fort Fisher

January 15, 1865

Late afternoon

From the bombproof beneath Pulpit Battery, Caleb made his way south, along the inside of the seaface. The sun had set, and only a dim twilight lit the parade ground, pockmarked with shell craters and littered with the debris of destroyed buildings. He heard musket fire behind him as bands of Confederates still offered token challenges to the Yankee bulge inside the west gate.

At the southern end of the seaface, Caleb turned left and hugged Mound Battery around the corner to the open shore on the other side. He then reversed course, creeping north along the outside of the seaface, staying in the shadows.

The open Atlantic was to his right, with the arrogant Yankee fleet plainly visible. The ships were arrayed in perfect battle lines, their smokestacks spewing fumes from steam engines tamped down for the night. Their guns calmly discharged the firepower the Yankees had brought to bear.

It seemed as if every ship in the Yankee fleet was still firing, although at a slower rate than in the previous two days. It was almost as if the fleet was toying with the fort, taking turns as to which ship would deliver the next devastating explosion. The bombardment had dismembered his fort, as well as the men within.

From atop Mound Battery three nights earlier, Caleb had watched the fleet arrive and anchor, and over the last two days, he had targeted ships during the fort's meager defensive efforts. Yet now, studying the armada from beach level, it appeared even more formidable. General Whiting had counted seventy-six warships, fifty-nine of which were gunboats. Propelled by the giant steam turbines that ate coal and belched soot, these modern gods of war spewed death and destruction on his home state—a collection of quiet farms and plantations serviced by a peace-loving and independent-minded citizenry. North Carolinians just wanted to be left alone, but these mechanized Horsemen of the Apocalypse would not let them.

How could he have thought that his collection of farmers, school-teachers, and shopkeepers had any chance against the industrialized might of the federals? Was it foolishness or vanity that had caused him to enlist?

There was one chance left for the dream of an independent North Carolina, and it rested on his ability to run. The ships' lookouts would never spot him, an indistinct shadow against dark sand walls, but he crouched nevertheless.

Past the Northeast Bastion, he continued straight up the beach. Any other day, the logical course would have been to cross the open plain behind the palisade to the river and then run up the open Wilmington Road. He had run along that road so often in the last two years that he was sure he could do it in total darkness.

But now, Yankees were pouring down the road into the fort to slaughter his fellow North Carolinians.

If this were midday, he would keep to the beach above the Yankee army's northern edge and then angle diagonally across the peninsula to the Wilmington Road. Once above enemy lines, he could run the last few miles to Sugar Loaf and General Bragg.

But this was not midday. Crossing among the pines in the dark would get him lost. Thrashing about blind in brambles would get him shot.

No, he would stick to the open beach and then, just below the Yankee encampment he had studied from the top of the Northeast Bastion, he would turn left across the peninsula, keeping south of the woods. On that part of the route, he needed to see where he was going.

That would still bring him out too far south on the Wilmington Road.

He would have to pick his way along the edge of the road, dodging Yankee reinforcements, until he was past their northern defenses.

He had no weapon with him. If he were confronted by patrolling infantry, he had no chance to fight his way out, and a weapon would only get him killed. If caught, he would claim he was a deserter going home.

One hundred yards north of the Northeast Bastion, he spotted dozens of mounds upon the beach, some lying in the ocean's wash.

He crouched and strained to identify the objects. When they didn't move, he cautiously crept forward.

They were bodies, remnants of the sailor attack. The Union graves detail had not yet reached them. They lay as silent testament to the battle's early hours. He rose back up to a crouch and began zigging between them when one cried out.

He turned. Twenty feet to his right, a Union sailor lay on his side. Each successive ocean wave washed over his head.

The sailor called to him.

Caleb looked around.

The sailor cried again and reached out an arm.

At first, Caleb thought the sailor held a weapon, but then realized he was beseeching.

Caleb hesitated. This sailor had come to kill him and destroy his state and its way of life. He had driven and fueled the machines.

Caleb had no time for this. He had to reach General Bragg.

Another wave washed over the sailor, leaving him coughing and sputtering when the water retreated. The tide was coming in, and the man could not move. In minutes, he would drown.

Caleb went to the man's side and dropped to his knees.

"Where you hurt?"

If the sailor recognized him as a Confederate, he gave no sign.

"Not bad. Just below right hip. I stopped the bleeding, but I can't move."

Caleb gently rolled him onto his left side. He could see no bloodstain—the ocean's ebb had washed the uniform—but he saw where the man's pants were torn and a kerchief had been stuck inside. Minié ball.

The bleeding appeared to have stopped.

When the next wave rolled in, Caleb lifted the sailor's head until the water retreated.

"Thank you," the man whispered.

"Where you from?"

"Delaware."

"Let's get you to higher ground. Can you walk?"

"I tried to stand, but I can't. Can't crawl neither in this sand."

Caleb put his arms under the sailor's shoulders and sat him up. He positioned the man's torso over his knees, and the man put weight on his left leg. Caleb helped him to his feet.

With the sailor's arms over his shoulders, Caleb was able to half-walk, half-drag him to the grass above the beach. Losing their footing in the soft sand, they tumbled together to the ground. The sailor did not cry out.

Caleb checked the wound again. It had not reopened.

"Can you feel both legs?"

"Yes."

"Arms?"

"Yes."

"Can you move the right leg?"

The man flexed his leg back and forth painfully but fully.

"I don't think it's broken," Caleb said.

"I just could not get up by myself," the man repeated.

"Have there been no stretcher-bearers down here?" Caleb asked.

The man nodded over Caleb's shoulder. Caleb turned and saw two Union soldiers picking their way along the sand, stopping every few feet to kneel and check the bodies strewn across the beach.

"You have to go," the man said, looking at him.

Caleb hesitated only long enough to pat the sailor's shoulder. He slid back into the deep grass. On his belly, he crawled away from the shore. When the two approaching medics stopped at where he had left the sailor, Caleb scrambled around them and back to the beach. When he saw more medics heading down the sand, he turned and made his way through the tall grass, away from the ocean.

He would have to cross the peninsula farther south than planned. But at least, below the pines, he could use what light remained to keep a diagonal course and come out as far up the road as possible.

Reaching the grass at the edge of the Wilmington Road, he looked both ways and listened. When he was sure no one was approaching, he stepped out and resumed his run north. He gathered speed and lengthened his stride.

Maybe he would be lucky and make it all the way to Sugar Loaf. Maybe, in the face of all logic, the Union Army had abandoned their northern line to reinforce the fort. Or maybe, even better, their army had called off fighting for the night, and no more troops would be marching down the road.

There was still enough twilight to avoid stumbling. Running at night was so much different than running in predawn light. In predawn light—

"Halt!"

He saw no one but instinctively stopped. Two Union soldiers rose from crouched positions on the side of the road and advanced toward him, rifles held forward. He moved his arms away from his sides. They stopped three feet from him, out of lunging range, their bayonets pointing at his chest. One soldier stayed in front of him while the other circled behind. Both were Negroes.

"Where you heading, Reb?" the one in front asked.

Without moving his hands, Caleb nodded up the road. "Home."

"Fleeing the battle, are you?" the one in front asked.

Caleb looked back toward the fort. "It's almost over. There was no reason for staying."

If they thought him a deserter, perhaps they would let him go.

"I have no weapon," he added when he felt the one behind reaching into his clothing.

"He's telling the Lord's truth, Jim," the one behind said. "He's got no pistol, nothing."

The one in front slightly lowered his musket. "What's happening in the fort?" the one called Jim asked.

Caleb moved his hands back to his sides slowly, but the soldier did not react.

"It's just about over. You Yanks have most of the northern wall and most of the parade ground. We are almost out of ammunition."

"Damn!" the one behind said. "Looks like they won't be needin' us none, Jim."

"You have a knife on you?" Jim asked.

Caleb shook his head. "No weapon. I was artillery."

This seemed to satisfy Jim, and he took one step back and lowered his musket to the ground. He was now farther out of lunging range, and Caleb had no idea what the one behind was doing.

"What's your name, reb?" the one behind asked.

Caleb told him.

"Any more of you, hereabout?" Jim asked.

"No, but I'm sure more will be leaving the fight now."

Caleb considered making a lunge anyway, trying to knock the musket away from Jim or grabbing it and turning it on the one behind, but it was much too risky. Even if he grabbed the musket in front of him, it was unlikely he could turn it before he was stabbed from behind.

"What'll we do with him?" the one behind asked.

Caleb heard it first. The faint clanking sound that rose in intensity. It was slung bayonets striking canteens, striking sword buckles. It was an army on the march, and it was advancing toward them down the road.

Skirmishers! These two weren't pickets, they were skirmishers for a detachment moving south to the fort. He was grateful he had not tried to escape. It would have been futile.

Around a bend, the army appeared, a white officer leading a Negro unit—in straight lines, marching wordlessly at a comfortable but quick pace. *Battle veterans,* he thought.

The officer stopped but motioned the unit to march past. Only an occasional soldier glanced sideways as they passed.

"Colonel Blackman, sir," Jim said. "Claims he's a deserter from the fort. Says things going poorly for the rebs, and there may be more of them heading this way."

The colonel nodded. "We have no room to take prisoners with us."

An approaching captain at the head of his company stepped to the side of the road as his soldiers moved past.

"These your men, Captain Pinney?" the colonel asked.

"Yes, sir."

"Very well. Detail two more to move ahead of the column. Accompany these soldiers back to General Paine with the prisoner. Then rejoin us at the fort."

The captain saluted and moved off, calling on other soldiers to advance double-time to the front.

"You heard him, reb," the one who had been standing behind him said. "The war is over for you. Now we's got to march the other way."

CHAPTER 30

Fort Fisher

Outside the River Road sally port

January 15, 1865

Evening had come to the battlefield.

Patrick Sheedy sat splayed on the ground just outside Fort Fisher's western gate and opened his Colt Navy revolver. He was exhausted. He hadn't eaten since shipboard breakfast fifteen hours earlier, and now, despite the tension of combat, he was hungry. Next to him, a soldier from New York swore as he worked on the hammer of a Springfield rifle with a small tool.

"Damn thing keeps coming loose. Won't strike straight."

Patrick Sheedy studied the surrounding ground, littered with the discarded equipment and rifles of the killed and injured.

"Grab another one."

The soldier looked at him like he had suggested suicide.

"I can't do that," the soldier protested with a look of astonishment. "I've had this one since before Petersburg."

Patrick was tempted to tell him that he wouldn't be carrying any rifle long if it didn't work right but thought better of it.

The rebel bombardment from the battery south of the fort that had struck both sides indiscriminately had stopped. Patrick assumed that his Union Navy had knocked it out. After the first rebel counterattack across the parade ground, he had remained in line on the ground. He had witnessed the rebel cannon blast that had ripped into the Union line to his left, and he had seen Seamus Flanagan go down. He feared he was dead.

He had been unable to go to his friend's side, even after the enemy charge was blunted. During a lull, stretcher-bearers had raced to the spot, removing the dead and injured. Despite the Union numerical superiority in the yard, there had been no follow-up advance by his fellows. Instead, they remained in their semicircular salient, exchanging fire with pockets of rebels hidden among the debris and craters of the parade ground.

As rebel firing slackened, Union soldiers had dropped back from the front line to the gate in small groups to relieve themselves or restock their ammunition pouches. Crates of ammunition now lined the Wilmington Road where it entered the fort.

He had been firing his revolver across the yard from his prone position. It was a cap and ball Colt 1851 Navy model, chambered in .36 caliber. The cylinder had six chambers, and they were empty.

Reloading was not easy. Measured powder was poured into the front of each of the six chambers of the cylinder and then a Minié ball inserted in each. The revolver came with a ramrod lever attached under the barrel. Pulling the forward end of the lever in a down-and-back motion activated the ramrod mechanism, seating the Minié ball to the back of the cylinder. The action was repeated six times. When completed, the revolver was turned and a percussion cap inserted on each of the six nipple ends located at the back of each slot.

The advantage of using the revolver over a Springfield rifled musket was that Patrick could fire six shots by merely cocking the hammer and squeezing the trigger repeatedly, whereas the Springfield had to be reloaded after each shot. The disadvantage, besides its lesser accuracy at distance, was that it took six times as long to reload.

And now Patrick had an additional problem. His Navy Colt revolver was chambered in .36 caliber. The ammunition crates piling up behind him were filled with paper cartridges and .60 caliber Minié balls for the muskets. Patrick and other sailors had joined the army's surge into the fort after becoming separated from the main body of sailors, who had been routed up the beach. If the navy had landed additional ammunition for the Colt revolvers, it was still crated at the landing site.

He only had powder and shot for six last rounds, and he filled his revolver. Unless he took his own advice and grabbed a discarded musket, he would only have six more shots before he'd have to resort to his cutlass.

The soldier next to him still struggled with his Springfield. Other soldiers stood around, talking about the fight they had just left, about who was wounded or dead, and what would happen next. Some swung spades to dig a deeper defensive line on the parade ground.

Fighting continued along the wall, traverse by traverse. The Union now held over half the landface, and returning soldiers said the rebel field pieces at the sally port had been disabled.

Another brigade double-timed down the road toward him. There was little rebel fire on it from the wall. When the new brigade entered the gate, the commander announced that it was Abbott's. However, their soldiers did not immediately climb the wall to join the fight among the sand hills nor enter the fort to take up position in the parade ground.

Instead, they stood about, crowding the ones already digging in or relaxing. *They have no orders*, Patrick realized.

He looked for his fellow *Iosco* shipmates. He had last seen Nat Davis climbing the wall to fight along the traverses. He hadn't seen Vranken and Phillips since racing from the rifle pit. He knew other sailors had made their way into the fort, but none of them were in sight. He wanted to find Nat, to at least learn that he was uninjured. He had no idea how the other *Iosco* sailors had fared along the beach.

The sun was down behind the river, and the moon had not yet risen. Patrick doubted that the battle could be continued in darkness and assumed that the order would come for everyone to entrench.

Squinting up the road, he spotted yet another group of Union soldiers approaching. When they entered through the gate, he saw they were colored.

They, too, milled about, adding to the general confusion of swarming soldiers, who talked, laughed, or greeted acquaintances from other units. Some started cook fires, and others joined in digging. Colonel Albert Blackman's recently arrived 27th Colored Troops were dispatched back outside the fort to dig yet another line of defensive entrenchments. One regiment of Abbott's brigade—Colonel William Trickey's Third New Hampshire—was ordered forward, up the wall to the front, but only to relieve battle-weary combatants, who trudged back tired and hungry. The assault had bogged down.

A stir near the gate drew Patrick's attention. A general in full uniform entered the gate, accompanied by a colonel and a bevy of aides.

"That's General Alfred Terry himself," the soldier next to him said reverently, "and that colonel with him is Cyrus Comstock."

The group strode straight to General Ames, and a vigorous argument ensued. Ames wanted to entrench and wait for daybreak to develop a cohesive attack. General Terry was afraid that the rebels would reinforce the fort overnight and wanted the rest of General Paine's division brought up. Let the sailors hold the northern defensive line.

Colonel Comstock suggested a compromise. Keep Paine's division and the sailors in place, and organize the newly arrived soldiers into squads of one hundred to charge the wall in waves, keeping pressure on the exhausted defenders. Once the landface was taken, the Union force would turn south and sweep the rebels from the fort.

Terry agreed, and orders were dispatched. In minutes, two regiments were formed up near the gate. Patrick stood and approached an officer.

"The 7th New Hampshire," the officer answered in a booming voice. "I'm Lieutenant Colonel Augustus Rollins, and yes, sailor boy, we'll take all the help we can get."

The 6th Connecticut also formed up, and the two regiments double-timed along the inside of the landface, Patrick at the rear of the 7th New Hampshire. Sporadic rebel fire from behind their earthworks near the seaface kicked sand around them. As the two regiments came opposite the third traverse, rebel fire intensified, and the officers directed their soldiers up over the wall and down to the sheltered protection outside of the landface. From there, the two regiments proceeded single file, hugging tightly to the landface's outer wall. They passed below the last three traverses held by the rebels until they reached the bottom of the Northeast Bastion.

Above them, rebel fire was waning, and soldiers whispered their fervent hope that the enemy was running out of ammunition. The moon had risen. In the dim light, Colonel Rollins organized the remnants of his two regiments into two lines. The 7th New Hampshire was positioned on the right and the 6th Connecticut to its left.

Soldiers in both lines stared up at the bastion. No one shot at them, and Patrick wondered whether any rebels remained on the parapet or whether they had committed to the fight along the traverses.

He turned and tried to see the beach. Hours before, he had crouched and watched as his fellow sailors had been massacred—racing at the fort, waving their swords. By now, any bodies still on the sand would be tossed by the incoming tide. He tried to locate the spot where John Barber had fallen, the top of his head blown off by the now-silenced Napoleons.

He drew his revolver and squeezed it with his left hand. He had six shots, and when they were gone, he would draw his sword with his right.

"Silence," Colonel Rollins was saying. "No shouting. When we go, be quick up the hill, and kill any who do not immediately surrender. Right line first, and you Connecticut boys support us on our left. Once we make the top, clear any Johnny Reb who remains. Swing down behind those still fighting along the wall. No shooting until we've made the top and come up behind them. We can reload then. Ready?"

The men nodded wordlessly. Colonel Rollins drew his own sword, raised it high, and then, without another word, pointed it at the parapet looming above. He began striding up the grass slope.

The line moved with him, making an uneven charge. The hillside was steep, and in the darkness, men stumbled and fell, a few sliding to the bottom before regaining their feet. No one cried out. Patrick made as long a stride as he could as he struggled to keep up with the jagged assault.

The soldiers carried their muskets out in front but held their fire. When they were halfway up, a solitary rebel leaned over the sandbags and yelled something before disappearing back behind the wall.

"Faster!" the colonel yelled, and Patrick leaned forward and quickened his pace.

His mind jumped to the wall of gray that had poured murderous fire into his sailors that afternoon from this very wall, and he envisioned another deadly hail.

But none came. Atop the wall, the federals scrambled over the sandbags. Only a handful of rebels had returned at the shout of their comrade. A few got off shots before collapsing in a hail of Union musket fire. The blue line raced out of the bastion and swung right, toward the river. Hearing them approach, rebel soldiers defending the last traverse turned and raised their muskets, but the federals were too quick. Patrick fired at every rebel he saw until his revolver clicked empty. He drew his sword as a rebel charged him. Patrick raised the cutlass and was about to strike when the soldier stopped, threw down his musket, and raised his arms. Patrick pushed past him along the wall.

Although a few more isolated shots rang out, the rebels turned and surrendered. Shouts of "I yield" and "Your prisoner" filled the air.

Patrick slowed and then stopped. He breathed heavily. The battle for the landface was over, and already Colonel Rollins was dividing his troops into those who would escort the prisoners back and those who would begin a sweep south across the parade ground.

Lowering his raised sword, Patrick waited for his own battle energy to pass.

CHAPTER 31

Wilmington Road, north of Fort Fisher

January 15, 1865

Evening

"You men stay here," Captain Pinney ordered, "and guard the prisoner. I'm going to see Colonel Wright."

The three Union soldiers had escorted the rebel sergeant up the Wilmington Road, past the federal pickets. When they reached the Third Brigade's forward defensive line, the captain asked for the unit's commanding colonel. At a line of skirmishers west of the main Union line, a corporal had pointed the captain in the direction of Colonel Elias Wright.

"Captain," Jim Jeffereds called as the officer moved off to find the brigade commander of the 27th Regiment.

The captain paused and turned back.

"Yes?" he demanded impatiently.

Private Jeffereds trotted up to his company commander. He could tell that the captain was eager to turn the prisoner over to command and join the fight at the fort.

"Captain, sir, something's just not right here."

"What do you mean, Private?" the captain asked. He looked warily back to where William Carney lounged against a tree watching Caleb Cuthbait.

Jim knew he'd have to be quick.

"Sir, I've seen lots of boys running from a fight," he began. "Both sides. They're scared, they run. They keep looking back at the battle, afraid someone's after them. When you catch 'em, and I don't care if it's us or a rebel, they blubber about how they had to run, that their officers were fools and such."

"So?" the captain asked and bent to brush dust from his trousers.

"Sir, we was sticking to the brush so as not to be in the open. We heard this rebel coming afore we saw him. Then we seen him good for a distance as he come up. Sir, he was running easy and real steady-like. Every step in his run was the same as the one 'afore it. He wasn't hurrying. He wasn't looking back all scared."

The captain glanced back at the prisoner. Jim knew he was starting to get his interest.

"Then, when we caught him," Jim continued quickly, "he didn't offer up no excuse. Just said he was going home. He says he lives in Wilmington, but that be almost fifteen, maybe twenty miles. He gonna run that whole way, like a trained show horse?"

The captain turned full to his soldier and then glanced again at the prisoner.

"What are you thinking, Private?"

"Captain, sir. I'm thinking he weren't running away. I think he was running to."

The captain pondered. "Messenger?" he asked.

Jim nodded.

"Maybe. Yes, sir," he answered. "We checked his pockets good. There was no note, and he had no time to throw it away. I think he got it in here," Jim said, pointing at his head.

He now had his superior's full attention. Captain Pinney studied the prisoner carefully and bit his lip.

"Alright," the officer said finally. "We'll bring him to General Paine instead. You two men—"

The movement was sudden. Private Carney tumbled backwards. The wind was knocked out of him as he sprawled to the ground from the push. The rebel was into the brush before Jim could raise his musket.

The pair ran to where William Carney was picking himself up.

"He done cut to the left," William said sheepishly, pointing. "I think he's trying to make the road again through those woods."

"After him!" Pinney shouted. "You'll never get through those woods with your gear. Circle to the road and run him down. And don't come back without a prisoner," he bellowed at the backs of the two privates, who were already angling westward for the road.

"He's got himself a good head start," William said as they ran across the uneven sand.

"What happened?" Jim asked.

"I was just standing there, looking over at you, when he done give me a shove and sent me on my backside," William explained.

Jim swore.

"You know," William continued, "he coulda grabbed my musket and used the bayonet on me and then shot you or the captain."

"That boy got something else on his mind," Jim said. "Something's got his blood up."

At the Wilmington Road, the pair swung north, straining to catch sight of the rebel.

"You think he gonna keep running at that speed all the way to Wilmington?" William huffed.

Jim slowed to a trot. "I'm more worried about who else might be in these woods or hiding along the side of the road. Hoke's come down this way a few times. No tellin' when he be itchin' to try it again."

After several minutes, the pair slowed further, reducing their pursuit to a fast walk.

"Let's stick to the side of this road," William suggested. "There be more cover."

Jim agreed. "Keep an ear too," he said. "You hear anything at all, you let me know, and we go right for these trees."

"Only, in this dark, maybe any rebs think we be one of them."

Jim shot a sideways glance at his friend. "It would have to be a lot darker than this," he muttered.

William halted and studied the surrounding vegetation.

"You know, captain or no captain, we never gonna catch that boy," William said. "He too far ahead of us. We just gonna get ourselves shot. I say we give up and go back. Tell the captain he too fast. I think it's time to call it the end of a long day."

CHAPTER 32

"It's time to go."

Lieutenant Pinson stood between the cots of General Whiting and Colonel Lamb. In the hospital room beneath Pulpit Battery, stretcher-bearers and orderlies readied the wounded to be moved.

"The north wall is in Yankee hands," the lieutenant explained. "There are thousands of the enemy in the yard. Soon, they'll start advancing."

Colonel Lamb rose up on his cot.

"And Major Reilly?" he asked.

The lieutenant shrugged. "The last I saw, the major was trying to establish a defensive line. But all counterattacks have failed. We are vastly outnumbered. I don't know where he's at now."

"And General Bragg?"

The lieutenant shook his head. "Nothing yet."

The colonel stared off to the side. "And what is the major's plan?" he asked. There was still fight in his voice.

"His last order was to move everyone to Battery Buchanan—all soldiers who can still fight, the wounded, all the ammunition we can carry. With the protection of the battery's guns, we can make a stand. Preserve a foothold at the peninsula's southern tip for General Bragg to land Hoke's division and push the Yankees out of the fort. Or at least occupy them in the event the general decides to push south from Sugar Loaf."

Two stretcher-bearers arrived at the cots. Colonel Lamb lay back.

"I understand," he said.

The bearers stooped and lifted the two wounded officers. They were the last to leave the hospital room.

Patrick Sheedy and Nat Davis stood atop the Northeast Bastion and looked south. The moon bathed the parade ground in a brilliant glow. Rebel stretcher-bearers and small groups of soldiers emptied out of the shelters beneath the seaface and hurried south.

"Where they going?" Nat asked.

"My guess is, they're planning to make a last stand," a New Hampshire soldier next to Patrick said.

After the rebels on the landface had surrendered, Patrick had spotted Nat. Davis had been fighting along the traverses from the other side, and after the rebs' surrender along the wall, the shipmates had met up, rejoicing in each other's presence.

"Are you sure?" Nat asked when Patrick told him about seeing Seamus go down in a cannon blast.

"I searched the area, but the medical and graves people had taken away the dead and wounded, and Seamus was nowhere on the ground."

"He might just be wounded then," Nat offered.

Further information was impossible. The men of the New Hampshire 7th and Connecticut 6th formed up to sweep south across the parade ground to capture stragglers. The balance of Abbott's brigade was to advance south along the river's edge. The 27th United States Colored Troops was marching across the grounds below them with instructions to sweep south along the seaface, checking every bombproof in the wall. Their Union skirmishers had already disappeared from view, spread across the grounds in a line ahead of their unit. If the fort's defenders intended to put up one last fight at the southern battery, Abbott's brigade and the 27th would surround them at the peninsula's tip.

"What should we do now, boss?" Nat asked. He nodded at Patrick's holstered revolver. "You have any ammunition?"

Patrick shook his head. "I'm out. Plenty of powder's been brought up, but there's only bullets for the rifles."

"This fight is almost over," Nat said. "We done our shift here, boss?"

Patrick thought back to the rifle pits and his fellow sailors' charge across the beach after volunteering for a job that was not theirs. He thought of Seamus and his devotion to a government that fought for the little people. The rebels who shot him and the other sailors had stood atop the wall and jeered at his dead and dying comrades. His hand tightened on his cutlass's hilt.

"No, I am not done yet."

Nat nodded with approval. "Then grab you a musket," he suggested, indicating the ground around them.

Patrick shook his head.

"I don't want to take time to reload. Someone will shoot me when I'm pouring powder. My cutlass will do."

Nat looked hard at his friend. "I think it's more than that," he said simply.

Isolated groups of soldiers, separated from their own units, tramped south across the fort's interior for the final showdown. Nat and Patrick picked their way down the inner side of the landface to join them. The parade ground was awash with bodies and debris and pockmarked with deep craters. Occasional rebel stragglers were surrendering, and Union officers sent them back to the west gate under guard.

An isolated pocket of resisters in a bombproof fired into the parade ground. Soldiers from the 27th surrounded the doorway and demanded they surrender. When they did not, the Union soldiers raced in. A hail of muffled musket fire was heard from within, and then all fell silent. Their hands raised, three rebels emerged, roughly prodded by the bayonets of their Union captors.

"There may be more of them," Nat said. "Let's go down by the river, away from that wall."

The two sailors angled to their right, away from snipers who might be lurking among the ruins. When they reached the Cape Fear River, they turned south and walked along its shore, keeping a wary eye. Over on the west bank of the waterway, the isolated rebel batteries were silent.

They came upon Phillips and Vranken, kneeling over a fallen rebel who lay still.

Patrick had never gotten along with either, but seeing them now, and knowing that two of his shipmates had prevailed unscathed, gladdened him.

He was about to call out when Vranken briefly turned away from him to gather up items on the ground. In the moonlight, he saw Phillips emptying the rebel's pockets, spreading Confederate cash, a watch, and a pocket knife next to the body. Vranken picked up the knife, held it up, and opened and closed the blade. Apparently satisfied, he slid it into his own pocket before reaching into the other side of the rebel's pants.

"Hey!" Patrick called out.

Phillips looked up. "We found this one first," he said. "Get your own."

"What are you doing?" Patrick asked, his gaze moving from Phillips to Vranken.

Phillips stood. "What does it look like I'm doing, Fireman?" he sneered. "We ain't been paid for two months because of these lousy traitors who should all be hung. We're taking what we're owed."

"What's rightfully ours," Vranken said, still kneeling on the ground. He turned back to the body and pulled up the rebel's shirt. There was a gaping wound across the soldier's abdomen, and half his chest was open.

"He's dead," Patrick stammered.

"Well of course he's dead," Vranken scoffed. "Good riddance to him and his kind."

This was not what Seamus was fighting for. "You can't rob the dead."

"Oh, aren't you high and mighty," Phillips spat, turning to face him. "Or maybe you're disappointed he had no coal shovel on him you could use?"

Patrick felt Nat's hand reach out and cover his own sword hand.

"There's not a man here has more reason to kill the Lords of the Lash," Nat said evenly. "But once a man is dead, traitor or no, his soul done belong to the Lord. And his earthly possessions belong to his wife and children, for they be theirs now."

Patrick noticed that Nat had tipped his musket, its butt resting on the ground, just a little bit forward. Vranken and Phillips turned their attention to the musket also. They were unarmed.

"Looks like the nigger thinks he's a preacher," Vranken sneered.

"I ain't no holy man," Nat said. "I'm just a sailor in the Union Navy, same as you. But I ain't no pirate."

Vranken stared hard, and for a moment Patrick feared he was going to rise up and swing at his friend, musket or no.

"Let's go," Phillips said instead. He grabbed Vranken, pulling him to his feet while keeping his attention on the musket. "We're done here."

The two turned and walked off toward the seaface. Patrick and Nat watched until they disappeared in the gloom. When they were out of sight, Nat turned.

"Next time I suggest you grab a musket, you listen good. You never know where the enemy be."

"Aye. We'll need to keep an eye on them back on ship," Patrick said.

"That won't be no different now, boss, will it?" Nat said as they resumed their walk south. He chuckled. "But we got more niggers and Micks than they got pirates."

The pair passed more rebel bodies. The graves detail was fanning out across the parade ground and sifting through the debris, lifting and carrying the dead from both sides. Patrick took it as a sign that the battle was nearly over.

Near the wharves jutting into the Cape Fear River, three soldiers from Abbott's brigade had captured a rebel soldier. He didn't look old enough to serve.

They were from the Connecticut 6th, and they recognized their new sailor friend.

"You should give this boy some sailor lessons," a soldier joked to Patrick as he approached. "Claims he was trying to row up the river, but you need a boat for that, and he don't got one."

The other men from the 6th joined in laughter.

"How old are you, boy?" Nat asked the young rebel soldier.

"Fourteen, sir," the lad answered defiantly.

One of the Connecticut soldiers whistled. "They be taking them pretty young in your rebel army."

"You trying to get home?" Patrick asked the lad.

"Nah," a Union soldier answered for him. "Says he was sent down to find a boat to row up the river and tell the rebel generals to send down more men. But when he got down to the point, all the boats was already taken by the rebels from that battery. They spiked their cannons and rowed away before we could capture it proper. So he come back here, still looking for a boat when we caught him."

"A brave lad," another soldier said with earnest admiration. "But we'd have licked them down there too."

Despite the bravado, Patrick discerned relief in his fellow soldiers' voices. If the rebels had spiked their cannons and left, this battle was truly over.

"That true?" Patrick demanded, turning to the lad. "Don't lie to me."

"God's own truth," the boy answered.

Confirmation soon arrived. A messenger raced north past the group, shouting the news. The rebel major in charge of the fort had surrendered down at the tip. He had intended to put up a fight at the battery, but there were no guns or soldiers left. As their young rebel prisoner claimed, the battery soldiers had all skedaddled.

Word spread faster than the messenger could run, and soon loud huzzahs broke out from all corners of the shrouded parade ground and from atop the fort's darkened walls. The word spread to the fleet. Within minutes, the anchored ships began firing signal rockets in a massive, impromptu fireworks celebration. Shouts of jubilation from their sailors wafted across the water to the parade grounds.

"That's a signal alright," Nat said as the Union soldiers inside the fort craned their necks skyward to watch the bursting signal rockets. "A signal that this fight is done over."

CHAPTER 33

Wilmington Road, north of Fort Fisher

January 15, 1865

Late evening

Caleb had easily outdistanced his pursuers. His frequent runs up the peninsula had helped him gain stamina and acquire familiarity with the terrain. Burdened by the weight of their weaponry, the Union soldiers had been no match for his endurance.

But he knew that those two would not give up—especially as they suspected him of carrying a message. The taller one was smart, and they were determined veterans. There might also be Yankee patrols or pickets ahead. Scampering along the riverbank would leave him too exposed. He would have to get off the road and work his way through the pine and thickets in the dark, and then his pursuers would have the advantage in speed.

He was nearly at Elizabeth's cottage. She should be safely in Wilmington, but perhaps she had left behind her husband's rifled musket. He remembered it as an Enfield, and he recalled where she kept the powder and shot. He wouldn't have to deal with a Yankee regiment or skirmish line this far north, and he knew he could no longer talk his way out of any confrontation. If the pair caught up to him, or if there were more pickets, he would have to shoot his way free.

He trotted around the final curve and was surprised to see flickering light from both the downstairs windows and from her upstairs bedroom. Why was she back? As he drew nearer, he slowed. The front door stood wide open, despite the cold night air. An involuntary shiver descended his spine.

Yankee scavengers, he thought, and his fear from December returned.

He stepped cautiously onto the porch, avoiding the board he knew creaked. He paused at the open door, listening, and heard a muffled commotion from the second floor. He stepped inside. Elizabeth appeared on the landing at the top of the stairs, struggling with an unseen assailant still inside her bedroom.

"Hey!" Caleb yelled without thinking. He leapt for the stairs. *Those damn Yankees.*

She tugged away, ripping her dress. A figure grabbed her and pulled her out onto the landing. A second man appeared behind him. They both wore tattered CSA uniforms.

Caleb shouted. "What are you doing?"

The first man turned and shoved Elizabeth back into the bedroom, releasing her as he did so. She slammed the door shut.

Caleb climbed the last step. "What is going on here?" he demanded.

They weren't Yankees, and they weren't from the fort. The uniforms were too dirty to identify. Two privates. *Deserters? Hoke's men?*

"You're just in time . . . Sergeant," the first one snarled, glaring at Caleb's arm patch.

He held a long knife at his side and the second man a length of rope. Caleb recognized it as the lunge line from Elizabeth's horse.

"This woman is a widow," Caleb said, trying to muster authority, "and a friend of . . . my family's."

"Really?" the second one asked. "A Yankee spy is a friend of the family of a Confederate soldier?"

"You should choose your friends better, Sergeant," the first one said.

The first held the knife in a thrusting grip aside his leg, with his thumb along the handle. The second appeared unarmed. Both men leered.

"I asked what you are doing," Caleb repeated. He tried to maintain eye contact with the one he perceived as their leader.

"You're just in time to help us hang a Yankee spy," answered the first one, tapping the knife absently against his leg.

"What are you talking about?" Caleb asked in disbelief. "I know her. She's not a spy. She's a seamstress here on the peninsula."

"Well, I guess we know her a little better than you. We seen her with a blue-suit colonel yesterday, right here in front of this house. But if you know her so well, maybe you're a traitor too and oughtta swing." He glared suspiciously at Caleb.

"That's right, Seth, you tell him!" the smaller man said, still holding the rope while remaining behind the first.

"Ain't you from the fort?" the first one asked, now studying Caleb's uniform closer.

"Iffin' y'all could fight better, we needn't got ourselves shot up trying to do your job," the second one said.

"And Asa still be alive," the first one added.

"Mebbe he's a spy too, Seth," the second one said. "Let's get her."

Turning, he threw his shoulder against the door, breaking it at the jamb. The door swung open. Elizabeth had moved a chest of drawers aside and stood at the far window.

"Where ya goin', Yank?" the first one taunted. "A little spitfire, ain't she?"

Caleb pushed past them, coming between the pair and Elizabeth. He turned and faced his fellow soldiers.

"I have an important message for the general," Caleb said, hoping the reference to authority would curb the bloodlust he saw in their eyes.

Without looking back, he asked, "Elizabeth, is this true? Are you a spy for Yankees?"

He assumed the answer would mollify the intruders. But what he heard was passion.

"I don't deny what I've done," she said from behind him. "I'm proud of it! I never hid who I am or what I feel from you. Look to your heart, Caleb, and you will know I have done right for myself, for you, and for our country."

"See?" the first one sneered. "A confession."

He pushed past a stunned Caleb and, grabbing Elizabeth roughly by the arm, led her into the hallway. They started down the stairs with her.

"Wait!" Caleb barked. He raced into the hallway. They were halfway down. "What are you going to do with her?"

"What we do with all spies, in every war," the first one, called Seth, shouted back without turning. "Hang 'em."

He gripped Elizabeth with his left arm, the knife at the back of her right shoulder.

Caleb followed downstairs, catching up as they reached the hallway.

"You can't just hang her," Caleb argued. "I'm on my way to General Bragg at Sugar Loaf. Come with me. She can be held and tried. You can tell your side, and she can tell hers."

The second one howled. "You're a fool! The woods are crawling with Yankees. Once that fort falls, they will be steaming upriver. You go run on up that road. We have done all the judging and are fixing to carry out the sentence. But we gonna have a little fun with her first. Spoils of war. After that, we figga' to find ourselves a skiff and get across the river."

"Deserters," Caleb said. His resolved stiffened. "Rapists and deserters. I won't let you hang her," he added softly.

The first man turned to face him, keeping Elizabeth between them. Raising the knife in his right hand, he shoved Elizabeth toward the kitchen with his left. The second man, still holding the rope, grabbed her.

"Keep an eye on her," the first said, "while I help this feller see the light. Or mebbe let the light into him a bit. He from the fort, mebbe someone need teach him how to fight."

He smiled wickedly and swept the long knife back and forth. Then, like a striking snake, he lunged forward, slashing at Caleb's thigh. Caleb stumbled sideways, falling over the footstool, and landed roughly on the rug in front of the hearth.

The assailant roared triumphantly. "This is for Asa! You will be avenged!"

As he stepped toward Caleb, two figures crashed through the open doorway, muskets leveled. From the floor, Caleb recognized his former captors.

The second Confederate soldier dropped the rope, shoved Elizabeth at the Union soldiers, turned, and raced to the back of the house. Private William Carney stepped to his left, aimed, but did not fire. Caleb heard the rear door smash open.

"Still can't shoot a man in the back," William Carney announced quietly. "Even a rebel. And a rapist, from what I could hear," he added, studying Elizabeth's torn dress.

In the parlor, the tableau was frozen. Caleb lay quietly on the floor, his eyes darting from Jim Jeffereds's face to Seth Colburn's. Jim had the drop on the rebel, who faced him with the long knife. It seemed forever before the Union soldier spoke.

"Well, mister, you can drop that sticker and come quiet-like, or I can shoot you."

Caleb could see the bloodlust still running high in Seth. His eyes were wide, and his chest heaved. Elizabeth and William Carney came into the parlor behind Jim as Seth raised his arm and took the first step. Carney fired, striking Seth high in his chest. The rebel dropped the knife and fell to his knees, grabbing at his shoulder. A thin stream of blood flowed between his fingers and down his dirty tunic.

Jim turned and, lowering his own musket, smiled. "Captain told us to come back with a prisoner. This one can walk. That one we would have to carry," he said, nodding at Caleb.

William Carney snickered back. "I see your wisdom. We fightin' this war so's we don't got to carry the white man no more. Might as well start tonight."

William set about reloading his musket as Jim prodded Seth with his.

"Get up, Johnny Reb. Your war is over."

Jim Jeffereds studied Elizabeth, who now knelt beside Caleb. She had pulled a piece of white cloth from her sewing basket and was wrapping it around Caleb's thigh.

"Caleb, hold this. I'm going to get some water to clean that gash, for a start." She stood and stopped in front of the Union soldiers.

Jim Jeffereds smiled. "He weren't no messenger, William. He was just coming here to protect his woman. As I'd want to protect Sally."

He looked around the cottage and nodded approvingly as Elizabeth busily pored through a sewing basket near the fire.

"And by the sight of things, he done got here none too early."

"Ma'am," Jim continued softly, "I think there might be a lot of men with guns coming by here the next few days, so you might want to close your shutters and bar the door, and keep y'all heads down." He nodded toward Caleb. "We ain't gonna worry about that feller. His war is over too."

Privates Jeffereds and Carney got Seth Colburn to his feet and led him out of the house. They closed the front door behind themselves.

Elizabeth got Caleb to his feet and helped him to a chair by the window. From there, they watched the Union soldiers march their prisoner down the road and into the night.

Elizabeth took Caleb's hand and smiled. "You foolish man, facing down two soldiers to protect me. I imagine it's going to take quite some time to get you properly fixed up, but I think you'll be worth it."

Caleb struggled to sit up. "It's over, isn't it? All of it." When she didn't answer, he shook his head. "I mean, the whole thing—the secession, the fight for our state, the war . . . All of it, gone."

She ripped his trouser leg open wider and wiped at the blood. She studied the cut and then, rising, retreated to the kitchen before returning with a pitcher. She poured water onto the wound and wiped some more.

"What will we do now, North and South?" He winced from the pain as she dug into the wound with the cloth. He propped himself with his elbow and shook his head.

"I don't know if it's over," she said without looking up at him, "so much as just beginning."

Caleb shook his head. "It's not proper for me to stay here in your cottage." He paused. "Unless . . ."

"Unless what?" she asked, sounding confused but still focused on the wound.

He pulled his grandmother's ring from his pocket. "Unless we are to be wed."

"Lie back and hush up," she said, leaning forward and applying a thick cloth to the wound. "I am going to give you some whiskey, and then I'm going to finish cleaning and sew up that leg. Like those soldiers said, our war is over too, and we're going to stay together until you're well. And I suppose if accepting God's gift and marrying you is what it will take, then so be it." She leaned in closer and kissed his cheek. "Don't go anywhere."

As he watched her leave the parlor, he realized there was nowhere else he wanted to be.

CHAPTER 34

Fort Fisher

January 15, 1865

Late evening

Sailors and soldiers wandered across the parade grounds and milled about Mound Battery at the southern edge of the fort. Some stopped to pick up souvenirs—bayonets, canteens, and even a few revolvers. Others rummaged through the bombproofs, looking for alcohol. The rebel prisoners had been assembled back at Pulpit Battery, and stretcher-bearers carried the wounded from both sides to the hospital room below.

Patrick did not want to exit via the western gate or sally port and have to walk past the rifle pits. He and Nat circled around Mound Battery, now looking puny in its abandonment, and turned up the beach in front of the once-imposing seaface.

"They called this the Gibraltar of the New World," Patrick said as he studied its grassy slopes.

"What's that?" Nat asked.

Patrick shrugged. "I don't know," he admitted. "Some big fort in Europe, I think."

The fleet rocked gently to his right, lit by the moon. As he walked past each gun emplacement, he noted the cannons, toppled and smashed, and marveled at the power of his fleet.

He spotted the *Iosco*, the last ship in a line that stretched to the south. Smoke wafted from its solitary smokestack, and he idly wondered who was on duty, keeping the boilers at half-steam.

His views of the fleet had always been from the deck of his ship. Shore leave was rarely allowed in the Union Navy, such was the fear of desertion, and he drank in the view.

It was a cloudless, starry night, and the smoldering boilers of the fleet were easily identifiable by the shadow their smoke cast against the sky.

"Look at all the steam engines out there," Patrick marveled as they walked north. It was just past high tide. The foam of breaking waves gleamed. "Everything will be different, Nat," he said.

"What do you mean, boss?" Nat asked.

Patrick gestured seaward.

"The war will be over soon, and this country is changing. Those boilers, steam, why, it won't just be jobs for us laboring on a farm someplace, sunup to sundown. Steam is the future, and there'll be plenty of uses in the coming years. Jobs, good jobs. Jobs for people like us. I come from another country. You come from a plantation. But they'll need us, Nat, not just to pick cotton or hoe a field, but to work. In cities. This steam, it won't just power ships. It will power all of us."

North of the fort, the pair picked their way along the beach. The stretcher-bearers and graves detail had completed most of their grisly work, and the wounded and dead had been removed.

In the distance, Patrick saw a group of men near where he had landed that morning. They had lit a bonfire that grew in intensity as he and Nat approached. Men dragged fallen limbs and threw them atop the flames. They were singing.

As he neared, Patrick saw that the men were all sailors.

The pair halted as Ensign Jameson hurried up to them.

"My God, where have you been?"

Patrick was confused by the question.

"We was stuck in the pits when the attack started," Nat explained. "We entered the fort with some other sailors and done fight with the soldier boys."

"Well, thank God you're safe," the ensign said, obviously relieved. "I was afraid I'd have to amend my count."

"Count?" Patrick asked.

The ensign indicated a tablet he held in his left hand.

"Killed and wounded. From the *Iosco*. Only John Barber and James Madison were killed today. You two were the last I hadn't heard from."

"James Madison?" Patrick asked. "Are you sure, man?"

"Aye," the ensign answered. He appeared offended at having been challenged. He shook the tablet. "I have all forty-four of us. Well, leastways, forty-two until you two showed up. James was killed in the attack along the beach. And John Barber, he was killed from a grapeshot from the sally port."

"Seamus, Seamus Flanagan," Patrick said, hope rising. "I saw him go down in the fort."

The ensign checked his list again. "He ain't killed, and he ain't wounded. And I talked to all the men. Least, now that you two are here. And you don't look wounded to me."

"Who you asking about?" Ensign Feilberg demanded, approaching the trio.

Ensign Jameson turned to his fellow junior officer. "He was asking about his Mick friend, Seaman Flanagan."

Ensign Feilberg pointed back at the bonfire. "He was up there, asking about you two."

Patrick and Nat turned and raced to the fire. Seamus spotted them first.

"You're both alive!" Seamus screamed as they approached.

"I could say the same. I saw you go down inside the fort."

Seamus's demeanor darkened.

"Aye, I did. The lads took a pounding from that rebel cannon. And what a mess it was. I carried many back up to the field hospital and then stayed there, helping as best I could. It was awful.

"And what about you?" Seamus asked. "I never saw you after that."

Rather than answer, Patrick reached out and hugged his friend.

The sailors had broken out into a chorus of "Battle Cry of Freedom." They didn't all know all the words but were able to fake it as those who did carried the lyrics. Someone had a fiddle, and there were two banjos looted from the fort, and the sailors danced about the fire as if drunk. Someone else had a Union flag, and at the line "Down with the traitors!" the sailors would turn as one and point toward the fort. And at the next line "And up with the stars!" the sailor holding the Union flag would thrust the pole he held with both arms as high as he could above his head.

Over and over they sang the song.

"Working off their battle energy," Seamus remarked. "Like a Sunday morning hangover."

"They be celebrating," Nat pronounced.

Patrick nodded solemnly. "It was a huge victory here at the fort."

Nat turned to him. "Victory? Nah, not victory, boss. Life. They be celebrating life. They done lived through this day, and that be cause enough."

Just before dawn, the three sailors walked to the water's edge.

"We have orders," Ensign Jameson said as he hurried past. "I need to gather everyone. The boats will be in soon. We're shipping out within a few hours. Patrolling rivers farther south, they say."

The ensign trotted off to round up the rest of the *Iosco's* crew.

It no longer mattered where they were going. This war would soon be over, and a new world would open.

On the coast of North Carolina, the weather was cold but clear. There was no rain, no storm. The sky lightened, and then, from the horizon, behind the Yankee fleet, a golden veil of orange expanded to meet the bright-blue sky.

AFTERWORD
& AUTHOR'S NOTES

Within hours of Major Reilly's surrender of Fort Fisher, the dominoes began to fall. When word reached Confederate President Jefferson Davis of the fort's surrender, he telegraphed a desperate query as to whether it could be retaken. It could not. The next day—January 16, 1865—Union Secretary of War Edwin Stanton visited the fort and celebrated the end.

Although General Braxton Bragg had preserved his army from the Yankee fleet in order to protect Wilmington, he must have soon realized that, without the fort, the port of Wilmington was strategically useless. When the federals finally marched north, they entered Wilmington on February 22 without opposition.

Without the ability to resupply his army, Lee abandoned Petersburg and Richmond on April 3. President Lincoln went to Richmond, and he insisted on sitting in Jefferson Davis's executive chair while outside the window a Union Army band played "Dixie." The president claimed that he always liked the song, but clearly, after four long years, there was more to it than that. Six days after Richmond fell, Robert E. Lee surrendered his Army of Northern Virginia.

It is the land battles that seared themselves into Civil War lore. Vicksburg, Antietam, and Gettysburg have been the subject of countless articles, books, documentaries, movies, and television references. The sailors and soldiers who fought together at Fort Fisher have so often, like the battle itself, been ignored.

Newton Martin Curtis, despite horrific facial wounds and the loss of an eye, survived the battle. He returned to his native New York state and pursued careers in and out of government, including two and a half terms as a Republican congressman.

Following Lincoln's assassination, Colonel Cyrus Comstock was named by President Johnson to the nine member military tribunal assigned to investigate and prosecute the conspirators. Originally pleased by his appointment, he was known to remark that "death was too good for them." However, he soon became disillusioned with the tribunal and appalled by the secrecy and lack of due process afforded the defendants. When his opinion that the case needed to be transferred to civilian courts to protect the defendants' rights became public, President Johnson replaced him.

In 1869, he married Elizabeth Blair, the daughter of Lincoln's Postmaster General. He completed a distinguished career as an engineer, both along the Mississippi waterway and on the Great Lakes.

Colonel Galusha Pennypacker confounded his doctors by surviving the battle. In March 1865, he was promoted to Brigadier General. At age twenty, he became the second youngest to ever achieve that rank in the American military. Only the Marquis de Lafayette was younger.

Colonel Louis Bell died the day after being wounded at the bridge. His body was transported back to his hometown of Chester, New Hampshire, and buried in the village cemetery. His father and uncle had both served as New Hampshire governors, and his younger brother would go on to be elected governor.

After the war, Colonel Joseph Abbott, the former Concord, New Hampshire lawyer and Manchester newspaper editor who commanded Abbott's brigade, settled in Wilmington, North Carolina. He started a Republican newspaper in the city and served one term as a United States senator. Although originally buried in North Carolina, upon his passing, his body was eventually disinterred and reburied in Manchester's Valley Street Cemetery.

General Adelbert Ames also survived the war and made sure to continue his very public feud with Newton Curtis well into their respective civilian years. His 1870 marriage to Blanche Butler—daughter of Benjamin Butler, the commander of the first Fort Fisher expedition, whose decision to withdraw was roundly criticized by Curtis—did nothing to dampen their mutual animosity.

At a February 1897 reunion of federal officers at Delmonico's Restaurant in New York City, the general gave an after-dinner speech about the Battle of Fort Fisher. The dinner and speech were well covered in the February fifth edition of *The New York Times*. Present in the audience was then-Congressman Newton Curtis. Ames praised his father-in-law, Benjamin Butler, alleged that General Terry (who had passed away in 1890) did little, and claimed full personal credit for the battle's success, going so far at one point as to state that it was General Terry who had wanted to stop the assault at the end of the first day while he, Ames, had pressed on to victory. He said that if Curtis had been more aggressive the battle would have ended sooner with fewer casualties. He told a reporter for *The New York Times* that Colonel Curtis did little at the fort other than pick up and fire a few discarded rifles.

An uproar ensued among the assembled officers at Delmonico's. Curtis had to be restrained on multiple occasions during the general's talk. When Ames finally sat down, no one applauded, instead rising as one and shouting for a rebuttal from Colonel Curtis. When Congressman Curtis rose to speak, he seethed, refused to make eye contact with or even refer to General Ames other than in the third person, and called Ames a coward. Later that year, Congressman Curtis delivered a more scholarly analysis of the battle before the same group. Their feud continued.

Despite fictional character Seth Colburn's mistaken belief, Asa King did not die in battle but was taken prisoner. His papers, detailing his experiences and describing the skirmish in which he was captured, are housed in the Lower Cape Fear Historical Society Archives.

Major James Reilly, who took command of Fort Fisher upon the disability of Colonel Lamb and who ultimately surrendered the fort, settled outside of Wilmington. In his later years, he was known to gladly tour the ruins with veterans from both sides.

General William Henry Chase Whiting was taken into custody and passed away on March 10, 1865, while still a Union prisoner.

Colonel William Lamb, briefly taken into custody, survived the war. He eventually became a Republican and served three terms as the mayor of his native Norfolk, Virginia. His papers are housed at his alma mater, William and Mary.

The flag carried to the top of the Northeast Bastion by Colonel Rollins's 7th New Hampshire is on display in the Hall of Flags at the New Hampshire State Capitol in Concord, New Hampshire.

The Loyal Union League was an organization of Wilmington-area citizens who remained loyal to the Union throughout the war and who spied for the North. General Weitzel described his December 1864 meeting aboard ship with the president of the league, but he never identified the president by name or gender.

The original earthen fort eroded with time. The area on which the fort was located is now preserved by the state of North Carolina as a historic site. There are educational exhibits and a visitor center.

Although this book is intended as a tribute to those who fought at Fort Fisher to preserve the Union and end slavery, it should be kept uppermost in mind that this is a work of fiction. It should not in any way be considered a historical source. If a reader is spurred to do further research on the topic, I have accomplished my goal. Anyone interested in learning more about the battle should review more scholarly works. There are numerous articles that can be accessed online, and the state of North Carolina maintains an excellent website devoted to the battle.

In addition, a number of fine authors have carefully researched and written about this battle and its aftermath, and those works are highly recommended. One of many such outstanding books is *Confederate Goliath* by Rod Gragg. *Union Jacks*, by Michael Bennett, provides excellent background information for those wishing to learn more about the life of the Union sailor.

One of the more poignant firsthand descriptions of the battle that I came across in my research was contained in a letter written to his sisters by a young naval lieutenant, John Bartlett, describing his account of the sailors' attack. I found it in *The Official Records of the Union and Confederate Navies in the War of the Rebellion*, compiled as a thirty-volume set, 1894-1922, by Congress. More than this novel ever could have done, it puts a human face on a titanic human struggle in our history.

I hope you enjoyed reading this book as much as I enjoyed researching and writing it. Although all my books are rooted in history, this is the first in which I attempted to faithfully track a specific historical event. I had a personal reason for doing so. My great-grandfather, whose picture adorns my office, served on the *USS Iosco*. As I worked on *Fort Fisher,* I would occasionally glance at his picture and ask him to help me get it right. Hopefully, for all those who served, I did.

ABOUT THE AUTHOR

 Greg Ahlgren is a criminal defense lawyer in Manchester, New Hampshire. He received his BA degree from Syracuse University and his JD from the University of Pennsylvania School of Law. He has been a criminal justice professor, a state legislator, and a political activist, and he has appeared as a frequent guest on both national and regional television and radio shows on true crime and historical issues. His books include the alternate history time-travel novel *Prologue* and the international thriller *The Medici Legacy*, and, together with Stephen Monier, he coauthored the true crime book *Crime of the Century: The Lindbergh Kidnapping Hoax*.

Recreationally, Ahlgren has been a licensed private pilot, an avid sailor, and a not-so-avid skier.

Greg can be contacted at GregAhlgren@aol.com and welcomes feedback and hearing from readers.

WWW.GREGAHLGREN.COM

Dear Readers,
If you enjoyed this
book enough to review
it for Goodreads, B&N,
or Amazon.com, I'd
appreciate it!
Thanks, Greg

Find more great reads at
Pen-L.com